Eden

J. Wilhelm

Copyright © 2026 by J. Wilhelm

Editing and Cover design: J. Wilhelm

All rights reserved.

No portion of this book may be reproduced in any form without written permission from the publisher or author, except as permitted by U.S. copyright law.

No part of this book may be reproduced in any form or by any electronic or mechanical means, including information storage and retrieval systems, without written permission from the author, except for the use of brief quotations in a book review. This is a work of fiction. Names, characters, places and incidents are either the product of the author's imagination or are used fictitiously, and any resemblance to actual persons, living or dead, business establishments, events or locales is entirely coincidental.

The author does not consent to any Artificial Intelligence (AI), generative AI, large language model, machine learning, chatbot, or other automated analysis, generative process, or replication program to reproduce, mimic, remix, summarize, or otherwise replicate any part of this creative work, via any means: print, graphic, sculpture, multimedia, audio, or other medium without express permission from the author.

Warnings:

The way that these characters deal with their problems, with their mental health struggles, it **is not** healthy. I tried to be mindful and delicate regarding a very serious topic, but the truth is, reality is *exactly* like this sometimes. People live the way these characters live, and deal with their pain in the exact same ways these characters do. It was a truth that came to me and demanded to be told. I don't condone any of their actions, and this story is not meant to romanticize any part of their circumstances. Proceed with caution, besties.

Specific Triggers: Suicidal thoughts, depressive episodes, homophobia, toxic family members, cult-like behavior, unhealthy coping mechanisms, and **a lot** of unresolved trauma.

Much love,

J

PLAYLIST

The View Between Villages by Noah Kahan
what are you afraid of? by Jessica Baio
a little more time by ROLE MODEL
End Of It All by DWLLRS
Rest Of Me by Isaac Levi
Blood Sport by Sleep Token
Restless Mind by Sam Barber & Avery Anna
Locksmith by Sadie Jean
better off without me by Matt Hansen
Indigo by Sam Barber & Avery Anna
Good Things Fall Apart by ILLENIUM & Jon Bellion
The Hard Way by Cameron Whitcomb
The Night We Met by Lord Huron
Work Song by Hozier
Options by Cameron Whitcomb
Weathervane by Hunter Metts
Already Gone by Sleeping At Last

Lydia, from the very beginning, Eden was meant for you.

I'm sorry.

And for you, my dear husband. For being the reason this book even exists.

I don't think I was given this heart for me,
I think I was given this heart for you.
-a.r asher

Chapter One

EDEN

I shift gears just before cresting the top of the hill. What's left of the sunlight becomes visible, causing the water on the road and trees to shimmer like glitter. I yank down the visor since I'd prefer not to be blind by the time I get there. The orange and pink hues swirl together beautifully in the clouds, tugging at that feeling of longing in my chest.

This. This is why I came here.

My jeep starts to stutter, so I pull my hand away from the steering wheel to I glance down at the dusty dashboard.

"Fuck!" I blurt out without thinking. I immediately glance up at the roof apologetically. "Sorry, Jesus."

My poor jeep sputters along until it's barely coasting. I guide it toward the small parking lot ahead, praying that I make it there. I try to get a glimpse of what the sign says, but all I manage to catch as I pass by is that it's some kind of state park. I use what momentum I have left to slowly roll into a parking spot that's facing the sunset. I shift into park, and plop back against my seat with a dramatic exhale. How the heck can a mechanic constantly run out of gas? I know I should check it. *I know.* I also know that I'm about to have to pay a hefty bill to have this thing towed to town since I don't know anyone around here to bring me gas. I'm alone. *Completely* alone.

I grumble to myself as I hop out of the jeep and tug on my phone until it finally slips out of my coat pocket. I grab my cigarettes and lighter from the center console before closing the door. The gravel crunches beneath my feet as I step around and hop up on the hood. My eyes keep darting to the colors splattered across the sky as I scroll through the browser on my phone. I go through four cigarettes as I call my way down the list of every towing company within a hundred miles. Only one answers. *One freaking person*, and he can't get out here until first thing in the morning.

"Alrighty then..." I whisper to myself as I slide off the front of my jeep. I stand there staring out into the horizon. I'm only a foot, *maybe two*, from the guard rail. Just on the other side of the metal railing is a steep cliff that leads to... well, nowhere, actually. It'd be so easy. If it weren't for the fact that my parents would inherit everything I have, I could just—

"Hey kiddo. What's going on?"

I snap around faster than I ever have in my life. A dude, *a man*, stares back at me, eyes full of concern as he inches toward me. I didn't even hear his footsteps. The guy is like a freaking ninja.

"Oh, h— hi. Nothing, just gonna take a quick trip to the bathroom," I reply as I point to the little shed at the end of the parking lot with worn paint indicating its purpose. "Then I'm gonna lay down for a little while."

His eyebrows pinch together before he glances back over at the entrance I just drove through.

"Damnit Sheila..." He mumbles as he pulls out his phone and starts texting someone.

"*Okay...* you have a good one." I offer as I push off the hood of my truck and take approximately two steps before he stops me again.

"Sorry about that. We're supposed to have a sign at the gate with our hours posted, but someone stole it last week. We're actually closing up for the night. I already locked the bathrooms."

"Uhh..." I glance to my jeep and then back at the guy. "I can't exactly go anywhere. She's empty."

"She?" He asks with a raised brow, seeming to catch on as soon as he asks. "Oh. *Oh.* Your vehicle. Gotcha."

"Yeah. So, I'm not going anywhere. At least not until morning."

"Oh. *Yeah.* No. You can't stay here."

Did this mother— I pinch the bridge of my nose between my thumb and forefinger as I try to calm myself. I'm currently sitting at over twenty-four hours since the last time I slept or showered. I have a vehicle with no gas. *Again.* I can't get a tow truck until the morning, and my entire life is in shambles. Can't this guy give me a freaking break? What does he want me to do? Push the thing just outside of the gate and sit on the side of the road all night?

"What do you propose then? I've called every tow company in the region."

"Buster?"

"Do what?"

"Real southern guy. Can hardly understand half of what he says. Calls his truck Betsy or something. Patsy? Daisy? I can't remember."

"Oh, yeah. Yeah. Daisy. He's the only person that answered the phone. He said that his daughter just went into labor so he wouldn't be able to get me until the morning."

His eyes immediately light up, making it impossible to ignore the forest green and golden globes that shine back at me excitedly.

"Cam? 'Bout damn time." He blurts out as he starts texting away— Wait. Nope. That's definitely a phone call. *On speakerphone.* Alrighty then.

"Grapevine musta gotcha." Buster says in greeting.

"You a grandpops yet, old geezer?" The guy in front of me asks with a chuckle as he holds his phone close to his mouth. I've suddenly realized that I have no idea what his name even is. Shouldn't he have introduced himself if he works here? I glance down at his shirt, looking for some kind of nametag or identification, but there's nothing. It's just a plain tan tee that reads 'wildlife reserve employee' across his chest.

"Not quite. She's in labor, but the baby ain't made it yet."

"Ah. Alright. Ya'll let me know if you need me to bring anything down to the hospital, alright?"

"Thank ya. I'll send you a few pictures when the baby decides to show up."

"Thanks, Buster. Tell Cameron that she's in my prayers. Oh! And I'm gonna take care of the guy that called you up at the park. Don't worry about picking him up in the morning."

"Will do. Thanks again, Dixon. 'Preciate it."

Dixon.

He hangs up the phone with a genuine smile on his face. His fingers fly across the screen, quickly typing out a text before shoving his phone into his pocket and looking back up at me.

"Where were w— Oh, yes. Your jeep." He works out before starting to walk toward the only other vehicle in the parking lot. "Let me see if I've got my hitch. I can borrow the trailer from the maintenance crew and give you a lift back to..." He turns back around to glare at me. Seemingly wondering whether he's just forgotten where I'm from, or if I hadn't even mentioned it. I hadn't. To *anyone,* for that matter.

"Willows." I reply with a nod, giving him the location of where I'm going rather than where I came from.

His eyes light up again. I swear, he has to be the most expressive person I've ever met. I'm not sure the guy could hide his feelings if his life depended on it. He should definitely stay away from poker tables.

"No way," he says as he steps back toward me. "We're practically going to be neighbors. Where at?"

"Really? Uh... lemme see." I reach in my pocket to pull out the scrunched-up piece of paper I have in there.

"Elm Street," I confirm as I look back up at him. He leans forward, glancing down at the paper in my hand.

"No way!" He replies with excitement as he pats my shoulder. "We're *actually* neighbors. Well... kind of. I'll be like two houses down from you."

Great. This is a wonderful first impression. I can see it now. Mechanic looking for a job, but his first interaction with anyone from the town he ran away to is of him completely out of gas and stranded at a state park at closing time. No one is going to hire me.

I'll probably be selling this house before I even get comfortable.

Well... maybe. I don't really *need* a job. I just enjoy working with my hands.

"*How lucky.*" I say, heavy on the sarcasm.

"*Ahhh.* Don't be like that. It's not a big deal. I'll go pick up the trailer and get a couple of the night shift guys to help us roll her up on it. Alright? I'll be right back. Don't move." He holds his hands out at me like I'm a wild animal as he backs away. He's acting like I can get anywhere important without a vehicle. Unless he thinks that I was about to... I glance back down at the cliff just a few steps away from me. I mean I *was* contemplating it, but I wouldn't have. Well, that's a half-truth. I *would*, but not with my parents still alive.

"Actually, on second thought..." he declares, his voice much closer than before. I turn back around, and he's there. *Right there*. He grabs my elbow with one hand and starts leading me to his truck. Everything seems to slow down and my eyes dart to his fingers wrapping around my flesh. There's an immediate explosion of nerve-endings, and my brain is trying to register the sensation that's muddling my thoughts. Fireworks and flares light up my body causing me to yank my arm away from him.

"What in the—" I almost demand.

His eyes dart to the cliff I was just debating before quickly jumping back to me. It's clear that we both prefer to ignore the obvious. At least, I do.

"*The bathroom.* You said you needed the bathroom. You can use the one in the shop while I get the trailer hooked up. Then we can come back and get her on the trailer so we can head home."

I notice, for the second time, that he called my jeep 'her' after he was completely confused when I did it. There's this weird tickle in my heart that confuses me, but I just nod in agreement. I really freaking need to pee.

"Great," he says with a smile as he lets go of my arm and starts leading me to his truck. "So, where are you from?"

"Mmm," I hum thoughtfully. "Somewhere I'd rather forget, honestly."

"I know what you mean," he says as he opens the driver door. He peers over the top of the truck at me until I open the passenger door and climb up.

When he slides inside, we buckle our seatbelts in silence, both staring out the windshield as he starts driving. It's awkward, to say the least. He's acting like

I'm going to take off running and bolt over the side of the cliff if he isn't within my reach at all times.

I shift in my seat anxiously. "I'm not a flight risk or anything. I wasn't going to jump." I blurt out.

His brows furrow as the truck slows, stopping in front of a decent sized metal shop. "But you wanted to?" He asks without taking his eyes off the dash of the truck.

"Yes," I answer honestly. "But I won't."

"Why?" He asks as he squeezes his hands tighter around the steering wheel and spins them around nervously. The leather squeaks under the pressure causing me to flinch. I want to reach out to him, to let him know that it's okay. That he doesn't have to worry about me. He was so happy before, and I don't like that he's upset because of *me*.

I debate telling him a lie, something more palatable, because trying to make new friends is really difficult when you're always telling the truth. People say they prefer the truth, but they don't. *Not really.* Lying is a sin though, and even though my faith has been slipping, I know I'm not gonna do that. I toss around the idea of a half-truth, which is what I normally use when people ask personal questions, but for some reason, that feels wrong with Dixon. I'm not sure why, but instead of some half-baked story that's only partially true, I give him the most honest answer I've ever given anyone.

"Because my parents are still alive."

He nods, accepting my explanation as if he understands the sentiment. I doubt he actually does, but he seems satisfied with my answer, finally letting his chokehold on the steering wheel go.

"If something happens to your parents, I know the odds of that are low, but... will you give Willows a chance first? I think you'll like it there. The people are great. It's like a big family, and I know they'll welcome you the same way they did me, you just need—"

"Unless there's some miracle that God has planned for me, my parents *unfortunately* have a very long life left to live. Much to my dismay."

He lets out this wild laugh that makes my lungs tighten in my chest as he looks over at me in shock. "*Do what?*"

"I refuse to give my parents a single thing, and if I die..." I explain with an unconcerned shrug. "Then they'll get more than that. *Way more.*"

He shakes his head in disbelief as he opens the door. "You're something else."

"So, I've been told." I whisper. *My entire life.*

Chapter Two

DIXON

I throw the vehicle in park and glance over at him. He's really fucking pretty. A sad kind of pretty, but pretty, nonetheless. His black hair is messy from sitting in a vehicle for a long time. I wonder how many hours he was driving. He refused to say where he came from, but I bet he came from farther away. He doesn't have any kind of accent, so I can't even make an educated guess. I like that though. It's kind of mysterious.

"You never told me your name."

He glances over at me, his head tilting to the side slightly, like a puppy when they hear a funny noise. "And you never told me yours, Dixon."

I can't help the way my lip curves up in the corner. He's witty and fun, and I think I'm going to enjoy having him around. I stick out my hand to introduce myself.

"Dixon Wakes," I offer.

He smirks back at me, the first real sign of happiness I've seen on him all evening, as he shoves his hand into mine.

"It's nice to meet you, Dixon. Eden Arbor."

Eden.

He quickly yanks his hand from mine, turning to push open the door before I even have time to blink. I have to scramble out of my side, chasing after him. He glances down at the crumbled piece of paper again, trying to decipher which direction the address he has written down is. What is he planning to do? Walk there and leave his vehicle behind?

"Wait!" I call out. "Let me grab some gas so we can get her off the trailer and you can make it to the station. You have enough money to fill up, right?"

He tears his eyes away from me and glances up at the sky. I peek up, but I can't see anything other than the same old stars and moon that hang in the darkness every other night, so I look to him again. He tilts his head back down and nods at me.

"Yeah. I've got plenty of money. Just enough gas to get me to the station is fine."

We both move around quietly, him trailing behind me, as I methodically navigate around my space to shuck off my work shoes and head toward the garage. His footsteps echoing behind me are different, but welcome. I've been telling myself that eventually I'd get used to being alone, but I still haven't. I moved to Willows a few years ago hoping to leave behind all the shit from my past, but that's the funny thing about life. No matter how far you run... you can't hide. I spent ten years, *ten*, hoping and praying that the person I loved would finally open his eyes and see that I was the one, but it didn't work. I have no one to blame but myself. Everyone told me. *Everyone* warned me. But I had hope.

That's my fatal flaw. Always a glass half full. Even when there's fucking water leaking all over the damn place because the cup is cracked on all sides, I *still* have that stupid hope. It something that I've been trying to break for the last couple of years, but funnily enough, I've given up hope on *that*. It's just a part of who I am, I guess.

"You should be good to get to the station. Want me to follow you there just in case?"

"Nah. You've done enough. Thanks for all your help." He replies as he opens the driver door. It takes a couple of tries, but she finally cranks up for him. He unzips the window and folds it in, one of my favorite features of the older soft top jeeps. If I had to guess, it's probably an early nineties model.

"Thanks again, Dixon. You saved me a lot of trouble." He pauses, staring off in thought, "*A lot*."

"No problem. I'll see you around, yeah?" I ask as I tap on his hood.

"Yeah," he agrees with a soft smile as he shifts into gear. "See you around, Dixon."

I watch as he backs out of the drive and heads the direction we came from. There's a little gas station we passed down there he can fill up at. It shouldn't take him more than twenty minutes to get there and back, so I'll check to make sure he made it home when I get out of the shower.

He shifts gears, the wind twirling around his hair as he speeds off down the road.

He's really fucking pretty.

Eden's vehicle was parked in front of his house by the time I got out of the shower, so I figured I'd let him get settled in for the night. Now that the sun has risen, and it's the weekend, I thought I'd go check on him. I was up before sunrise and I've been piddling around in the shop in my back yard for hours, trying to distract myself. I swore that I was going to wait until at least ten, but I'm only twenty minutes early. Totally reasonable.

I raise my fist, still trying to convince myself to knock, when the front door swings open. The shock on Eden's face probably matches my own. He's just standing there staring back at me as I gawk at him. Like... literally gawk. He's filthy. Dirt is smeared in the trails of sweat that cover his entire body. He's wearing holey jeans, and... boxers? Probably. All I can see are the jeans. Or rather, they're the only things that my eyes decide *not* to look at.

"H—hi," I stutter out as I point behind me to the dumpster. "I saw that they delivered this thing a couple of days ago. I was certain someone was going to demolish the place. I'm glad it's gonna be fixed up instead. I thought I'd swing by and see if you needed help with anything."

"Right," he says as he lets the full trash can he was dragging behind him plop down on the hardwood floor loudly. "I'll never say no to an extra pair of hands. I'm just trying to get all junk out right now." He says as he looks back over his shoulder.

"You really should be more gentle on those hardwood floors if you plan on keeping them." I say as I point down at them.

"Oh Je—" He shakes his head in frustration. "Please tell me that you're a carpenter and that God sent you to help me fix all this sh— danggit. Please tell me you know how to work with wood."

I can't help the smile that breaks out on my face. Passing up on that opening would be a dying shame. "Oh, I can work wood. *In more ways than one.*"

His brows pinch together in confusion, and I'm positive, like ninety-three percent sure, that he's never going to talk to me again. I definitely crossed a line. Right? He actually surprises me though. After a couple of seconds of contemplation, his eyes roam over my body and then his cheeks flush bright pink. He quickly forces his eyes away and shoves the door open farther.

"Well, I'm glad." He says before he wanders off inside. I follow behind him, curiously glancing around the house that's been sitting vacant since I moved here. It dusty, really *really* dusty. Every surface is coated in a thick layer with random streaks where other people's hands have touched over time. There's not a single piece of furniture aside from two tiny barstools that seem to be on their last legs. Literally.

"I wanted to start in here," he explains as he leads me into the kitchen. "These cabinets have to go."

I run my fingertips along the face of one of the cabinets and then open one of the drawers. It's quality craftsmanship, something that's pretty rare these days.

"You don't like them?" I ask as I glance up at him. "They're hardwood. Most stuff these days is all that MDF shit. These will hold up centuries after those turn to dust."

"Obviously," he replies with a chuckle. "They look pretty dated though. Don't you think?"

"I can sand these edges down into something a little more simple, if that's what you're worried about." I offer as I run my finger along the decorative flower carvings on the door. "It'd be super easy and probably save you a fortune."

He leans against the counter as his eyes dart around the kitchen. He pinches his lip between his fingers, tugging at them as he contemplates. He finally points to the other side of the fridge and glances over at me.

"I really wanted to add a pantry here," he points to the other side of the kitchen next. "Maybe a couple of extra cabinets on that side too. It would feel a lot bigger in here, and there isn't really anywhere to store things like it is."

I nod along as he explains his vision, trying to picture it the way he sees it, but I'm a visual learner. I tug my phone out of my pocket, pulling the little pen from the bottom to scribble out the roughest image you could probably imagine. It's chicken scratch, at best, but as he leans over my phone to watch me, he nods along happily.

"Yes," he says excitedly as he points to my phone. "*That.* That's perfect." He says as he looks up at me. There's a second, or an eternity, that we stand there just staring back at one another. I've never seen a smile quite like his. It's not subtle, the way he is. It's sunshine during a hurricane. It's bright, and blinding. It'll catch you off guard.

There's something magical about making a person that always seems so sad feel happiness. I want to bottle it up and tuck it away in my pocket for a rainy day. I could pull it out again when he's upset to remind him that there are moments where he's still going to smile, and that his smile will mean something to someone. *To me.*

He clears his throat and glances down at the floor before taking a step back from me. I hadn't even realized how close he was until his warmth slowly starts to dissipate, leaving a slight chill behind. I ache to move closer to him again, to feel the touch of another person. It's been such a long time.

As I move to step past him, I nudge him with my elbow playfully, causing him to look back up at me. "I think you just found yourself a carpenter." I joke.

I point to all the cabinets along the wall. "We can keep all of these. I'll just take the doors back with me and sand off these floral carvings to give you a cleaner look. I can make you a larger pantry for this side and a couple of upper and lower cabinets that match for the other side. After we have those in, I can take a few measurements and see how much space we have to work with for the island. You want to have at least a three feet—"

"*Ompf...*" His body presses against mine as his arms wrap around me. I glance down at him in shock. Until this very moment, I hadn't realized how much smaller he was than me. There's a few inches between us, just enough difference that as I finally wrap my arm around him, the smell of his shampoo wafts into the air I'm breathing.

I soak up the feeling of his warmth, just content to feel affection from another person again. I've spent so long trying to convince myself that I can survive on my own that I'd completely forgotten that platonic affection is really fucking nice sometimes. It's actually scientifically proven to cause changes in the human body, and I can feel it. The stress of life and work slowly melt away, leaving me the most relaxed I've been in weeks when he finally pulls away from me.

"Sorry, I... I guess I really needed that." He fumbles out bashfully as he steps back from me. "And I'm just really grateful to have some help with this. I usually have to do all this by myself or hire someone to do the parts I can't."

"I don't mind hugs. Or touching. At all. People use to complain that I touched *too much*, actually." I admit with a chuckle as I lean back against the island and cross my arms.

"Oh... thank goodness." He says as he lets out a relieved exhale. "Same. It's a serious problem. Other people despise it and I have no idea how to control it. It's like my body just gravitates to other people no matter how much I try to stop it. *I hate it.*"

I shake my head in denial. "Nah. The people here will love it. They're all huggers. And I *definitely* don't mind. Hugs, cuddles, whatever. I'm always down."

He chuckles sheepishly as he pushes off the counter and grabs a roll of paper towels. "We just met, Dixon. That's a bit fast, even for me."

"Nah," I reply with a chuckle. "When you meet the one, you just know."

He turns back at me, handing me a spray bottle of cleaner as his eyes wander over me with curiosity. I can almost feel the weight of his thoughts bearing down on him. There's a darkness behind his eyes that tells me exactly how many burdens he's been carrying around with him, and I hate that. I want to pull him into my arms again and tell him that he's safe with me. That Willows will welcome him with open arms, and he won't have anything to worry about anymore. That I'll make sure of it.

I don't though, because I've always been a coward. So, when he reaches out and offers me a roll of paper towels, I silently take them.

"Let's get to work then. Yeah?" He asks with a soft smile.

I smile back at him, nodding in agreement.

Stupid fucking hope.

Chapter Three

EDEN

The road winds around, trees towering over everything in sight. Evergreens are all I can see for miles on end, but the cool crisp air makes me miss the orange and red hues of the leaves that typically litter the ground this time of year. The weather is perfect. Which is the only excuse I need to have the top off the jeep as I ride up to the lookout. I pull into my normal parking spot, the same one I rolled into that first night I arrived in Willows, and shift into park. I sigh in relief as I open the door and crawl out.

I lean back, stretching my arms and legs before climbing on top of the hood. I've been working on the house so much lately that my body aches incessantly. I feel about ten years older than I actually am. I can't imagine how Dixon is feeling. He's thirteen years older than me already, so I know he has to be exhausted. He spends all day working and then comes home to help me. I should probably demand that he takes a break this weekend. Maybe I could convince him to take me to look at some furniture instead.

"Hey kid," he announces as he hops up beside me. He wraps his arm around my head and pulls it against his chest as he ruffles my hair playfully. "You must have missed me."

I can't help the smile that forms on my lips, but I try to push out of his hold anyway. "Hardly. You're the most insufferable person I've ever met."

His chest rumbles with laughter as he lets me go and digs around in his jacket pocket for a pack of smokes, no doubt.

"And yet, you came to see me at work." He retorts with sarcasm.

He pulls out a cancer stick and holds it up for me until I lean over and take it between my lips. My eyes meet his as he pulls out the lighter and unsuccessfully flicks it a couple of times. His eyes stay locked onto mine, so every time he actually manages to get the flint to produce a flame, it flickers out before the cigarette lights.

His green eyes sparkle mischievously, trying to tell me something, but I can't understand. I can never decipher all the things he says in the silence. I don't understand *anything* when it comes to Dixon Wakes. Only that he's here, and I'm here, and we both seem to be happy about that. The rest doesn't really matter.

"You might actually be able to light the cigarette if you watch it instead of me." I mumble with the cigarette still between my lips.

"Sorry," he whispers as he tears his eyes away from mine. I miss them on me almost immediately, but I never have to worry. Anytime I want Dixon's full attention, I have it. I never have to beg him, and I like that.

The cigarette lights on the first try.

"So, what brought you to the peak today?" He asks as he pulls out another for himself.

"I needed some fresh air," I reply boredly before I take a deep inhale. "The house was feeling stuffy." Which is only half true.

His eyes cut down to the metal railing that's just a few feet in front of us before quickly looking back up at the sky. I don't know how he knows, but he does. He *always* knows when I'm thinking about it. I haven't changed my mind. I'm still not doing it. Not anytime soon, anyway. I have a lot of money to spend, or two parents that need to die first. I'm still here until then, but I don't think Dixon believes me. That's okay though, it doesn't bother me that he questions it. At least he cares.

"Hey," I say as I lean my head against his shoulder and take another drag from my cigarette. "Instead of working on the house this weekend, do you think that you could take me to some furniture stores to pick up a few things with your truck?"

He glances down at me, his long lashes much more visible from this angle. I wish my eyelashes curled as perfectly as his. I lift my finger to my eyes, trying to push my lashes back higher. Maybe I could try a curler. Is that gay? Would my parents—

"Quit," he demands as he pushes my hand away from my face. "Your lashes are perfect."

I give him a weak smile before sitting up, trying to focus on something more positive. "Do you think we could fit a mattress and bedframe in your truck? I'm tired of sleeping on the floor."

He turns toward me, clearly appalled, before sliding off the hood of the truck. "You've been sleeping on the fucking floor? *For two months*?"

"Yeah," I shrug as I slide off the hood, too. I toss the filter on the ground and stomp it out with my worn leather boot. "My back is killing me. I feel like I'm your age." I joke as I nudge him with my elbow.

"*Ouch*," he gasps as he clutches his chest in mock pain. "That was a low blow."

He leans down to snuff out his smoke in the dirt, picking up my butt and pocketing both of them. I love that he does it every time and never complains about having to pick up after me. For some reason, I can never seem to remember that we're not supposed to be smoking here.

"You aren't sleeping on the floor all week, Eden. We'll go pick out something now. Come on." He says as he waves toward the driver side.

"Fuc—" I scowl at him. "*No*. We aren't going today. I said this weekend. Not when you've been working all day."

"I'm not letting you sleep on the floor again. Ever." He declares as he starts walking toward his truck.

"We're going to get you a bed, or you're staying at my place. Period."

"I'm not going furniture shopping after you've been working outside all day. *Period*." I argue.

"Then we need to go grab your stuff so that you can stay at my place for the rest of week." He says as he shoves his hands in his pockets.

Ugh. I groan in irritation as I jog after him. "*Fine.* Okay? Fine. Just until this weekend."

When I catch up, I slow down beside him, matching his pace. The farther we walk, the bigger the smirk on his lips grows.

"What?" I finally ask, utterly confused.

He looks over his shoulder, raising a brow curiously. "I was just wondering when you were going to realize that your ride is back there?"

I glance back, glaring at my jeep in disbelief, before turning back around and punching him in the shoulder. "You jerk. I hate you!"

I take off, sprinting back toward my vehicle.

"I love you too, kid!"

"See you soon, old man!" I holler back at him as I skid to a stop beside the driver side door.

He spins around, walking backward to yell at me. "If I don't see you within the hour, I'm coming to drag you out of that house, Eden."

"Eff off, Dixon." I joke as I yank open the door and climb inside.

"I'm not joking!"

We'll see about that.

I was totally kidding about finding out. I still rushed to get all my shi— stuff together and get over to Dixon's place. This house is too quiet when he isn't here anyway. It took me twenty-five minutes to get inside my house thanks to the old lady that lives on the other side of me stopping to talk as soon as I stepped out of my vehicle. Then I spent almost twenty minutes packing some clothes, all my devices, chargers, and everything else I might possibly need for the next few days. Then I decided to take a quick shower with what little time I had left. I swear, I've never scrubbed my body so fast in my life. It didn't really matter though, because as soon as I've managed to dry off and slip on my briefs, I hear him.

"Eden Arbor!" He yells as the front door squeals open and bangs against the wall. There's already a hole behind it, so it's not like it really matters. "I've come to collect my prize."

I chuckle to myself as I rush to the bedroom and zip up my bag. Within seconds, the bedroom door flings open, and he just stands there staring at me. I smirk at him mischievously as I stand up straighter.

"I just need a second," I say quietly. "I'm almost ready."

He slowly shakes his head. "I warned you, kid."

His eyes trail over me again, and I can't help but wonder what he thinks. Even though he hasn't explicitly said it, I'm pretty sure he's gay. I don't care; That's between him and God. I just wonder what his type is. Does he like guys my size? Guys bigger than him? Although, that would be pretty hard to find. He towers over most people, and his chest is so wide. I don't know if I've *ever* met a guy bigger than him.

He snaps out of his perusal, his eyes locking with mine.

"Like what you see?" I ask with a playful smirk.

He raises a brow, challenging me as he walks toward me. I can feel my insides starting to quiver the closer he gets, but I keep my feet planted, refusing to cower. He feels like the sun. Every step he takes closer to me, the more my temperature rises until all I can feel is this burning heat consuming me from the inside. As he slowly walks a circle around me, I genuinely believe I might perish, turning right to ashes at his feet.

"Well?" I prod impatiently.

He walks all the way around, stopping directly in front of me. He still hasn't said anything, so every tick of the clock has my anxiety growing. I try to prepare myself for his rejection by staring down at my feet. I think it would hurt a lot worse if I had to see his face.

He doesn't like that though, so he grabs me by the chin and forces me to look at him. His thumb gently brushes along my bottom lip, causing the heat inside of me to transform into raging flames that flicker against the inside of my ribcage angrily. His eyes track the leisurely movement of his finger before they lock with mine.

"You're the most beautiful thing I've ever seen, Eden. I'd be a fool not to."

I give him a soft smile, gentle and appreciative. "Thank you," I whisper as I close my eyes and lean my forehead against his chest.

"But you're not getting out of this!" He says as he squats down and lifts me over his shoulder. I yelp and kick my feet, trying to defy him in any way I can.

"Put me down, Dixon! My bag!"

He snatches it off my bed and heads to the hall. He has absolutely no problem carrying me down the stairs and through the kitchen. He stops at the fridge, slinging it open with my bag still in his hand.

"Why is there nothing but pickles in this fridge, Eden?" He chastises as he turns around and puts my bag on the counter.

"*Ummm*... because I like pickles?"

"Wrong answer," he replies as he reaches up and smacks my as— butt. Why is that word so childish? He smacked my ass. There. I said it. That's not even the worst part. The worst part is that my... I'm getting hard, okay? And I know he's going to feel it.

"Put me down!" I demand as I squirm around in his arm again. He doesn't budge. He just leans down, messing around with something in the fridge.

"Wiggling around just causes more friction. It's only going to get harder if you don't sit still."

"*Dixonnnnn!*" I whine as I slap my hands over my face in embarrassment.

"You act like every guy doesn't have the same problem, kid. It's biology."

"Please stop," I beg through my hands.

"How are you an adult that can't even talk about dicks? Where did you grow up? A cult or something?"

He has no idea how close to the truth he actually is, and I'm dang sure not about to tell him. It's not something I even want to think about, let alone *talk* about.

"Dixon!" I growl as I tear my hands away from my face and try to glare over his shoulder at him. He shoves a box back at me, nearly hitting me in the face.

"Hold that," he demands. I'm struggling here, so I shift my weight, trying to grab it from his hand without throwing him off balance. When I finally get ahold of it, I pull it down to see what he's handed me.

Oh. My shot.

"How did you know I needed this?"

He closes the fridge before grabbing my bag off the counter. "Do you not need it this week? I thought it was the right time. Is it next week?"

My eyes get blurry as I stare down at the box that I'm still holding with both hands.

"No, I do. I just— Thanks, old man." I say with quiet chuckle. "That's really thoughtful."

"Of course, Eden. Someone has to take care of you."

I laugh again, tucking the box under my armpit. Dixon heads toward the front door, seeming to forget that I'm in nothing but underwear. At least it's dark outside, so I doubt anyone will see us. Willows is super fucking quiet, and I really like that.

"What do you want for dinner?"

"I'm not that hungry, actually. I ate before I came to the park."

"Ate what? *Pickles*?" He asks sarcastically.

"No, asshole." I growl back. "I ate at the diner. Thank you very much." I reply defensively, crossing my arms. The box nearly falls from beneath my armpit, causing me to scramble to catch it.

Dixon's steps falter before he stops right in the middle of the sidewalk. "Did you just— Am I hearing things?"

I let out a sigh as I roll my eyes. "No, old man. Butthole doesn't have the same impact as asshole. It just sounds childish."

"Well..." he says as he starts walking again. "I was sure that you'd be carrying my coffin before I heard a full curse word come out of your mouth. I'm impressed."

I scoff. "Cussing is not something to be proud of. In fact, it's quite the opposite."

He's silent for a few seconds before he finally speaks again, "Does it bother you when I say them? Curse words?"

His question causes me to pause. I never really thought about it that way. My parents used to tell me that people only cursed because they weren't intelligent enough to use more creative words, but I think that Dixon kind of disproves that theory. He's super smart, *and* funny, *and* creative. He's definitely smarter than I am, and he cusses all the time.

"I'm going to work on it, okay? I'm going to say bad words more."

"Well, thinking that words are inherently bad is your first problem."

See? Super intelligent.

"I know that, okay? I just— it's how I grew up. So, it's going to take some getting used to."

"Alright," he replies confidently. "How about this? Repeat after me."

"Okay," I say with a determined nod.

"Fuck whoever the fuck taught me that shit."

I immediately bust out laughing, which causes him to laugh, too. My stomach starts to ache, so I take deep breaths trying to calm myself.

"I *am not* saying that."

"You agreed. Let me hear it, Eden Arbor."

"Not happening," I reply with another chuckle. Man, what my parents would say if they knew I was hanging out with someone that just said those words.

"Eden," he growls in irritation. "Say the damn words."

"Fine!" I pout as I cross my arms again. "Fuck my parents for teaching me that shit." I say quietly. It feels oddly freeing, like breaking out of their shackles, and I can't help the smile that it brings to my face. Nothing is going to happen to me anymore. I'm here. On my own. *I'm free*.

"That's not *exactly* what I said, but I'll take it." He says as he turns down his driveway.

"You know..." I take the box from under my arm and spin it around in my hands as I stare off in the distance, watching a car's taillights as it disappears down the road. "No one believed me when I said something was wrong. They told me that I was just having growing pains. After I stopped growing because I was practically an adult, they would just say that I must have hit my hands or something because I was the clumsiest person they'd ever met. I knew that something was wrong though. *I knew.* When I left, the first thing I did was go to the doctor. That's when I got diagnosed. They said if I would've waited much longer that I could've had permanent damage to my joints. That really scared me. What else would've happened to me if I *didn't* leave, you know?"

"Eden..." he says as he leans down and drops both me and my bag on his front porch. He grabs my face between his palms. "Listen to me. *I* will always believe you. Okay? *Always.*"

No matter how hard I try to fight it, my view becomes blurry with tears. They try to run down my cheeks but have to fight to find their way around his fingers. His eyes bounce back and forth between mine, hoping that his words sink in. I want them to. I really wish they would... but they won't. As I try to nod anyway, the little droplets find their way to my lips, leaving that bitter, salty taste behind.

"None of that matters anymore. Okay? Just this. *Just us.*" He demands.

That, I believe.

Chapter Four

DIXON

Eden nods, this time with a little more confidence. I can tell he still doesn't feel my words as deeply in his soul as I want him to, but it's a start.

"That's my boy," I praise as I pull his head against my chest. I suck in a breath, the scent of him flooding my lungs. It's minty and herby, smells of nature that I've started to crave. I lean down to gently kiss the top of his head before I snatch up his bag and grab him by the hand. I lace my fingers between his, hoping that he doesn't pull away from me. I know that this could be considered crossing a line, but I don't mean anything by it. I swear.

Eden needs me tonight just as much as I need him, and I desperately want to feel that connection. I just want to strip down to nothing and lay beside him. I want to feel every inch of his skin warming my soul. I want to feel his legs mingling with mine beneath the sheets. The bristle of his fine leg hairs tickling my flesh. The whisper of his touches all over my body when I wake up in the morning. More than anything, I want to crawl into my bed next week and feel his ghost there with me, because being away from Eden has become the worst form of torture I've ever experienced.

I lead us inside, pulling my keys from my pocket and tossing them on the countertop as we stop in the kitchen. I open the fridge and wait as he throws the box of medicine inside carelessly. We'll have to find it a permanent home later. I push through the bedroom door, pulling his bag off my shoulder and dropping it to the floor. I let go of his hand as I move further into the room and reach for the hem of my shirt, yanking it over my head. He watches my every movement carefully. Cautiously. I kick off my shoes at the end of the dresser and then fully turn back toward him.

"Holy fuck," he whispers in awe as his eyes dart along every part of my body as if he's trying to memorize every wayward scar or the dips and curves of my physique. The way he looks at me is completely foreign. It's not full of hunger or lust the way men from my past saw me, because I'm not a hot night between the sheets for him. His eyes are sparkling with awe, but there's so much adoration and trust staring back at me that it almost makes me choke up. My heart feels so fucking full, and before I even have time to stop it, I've realized that this... this is it for me. I may never have a physical relationship with Eden, but as I stand in my bedroom with only feet between us, I feel more fulfilled than I ever have because of sex. I don't need that to be happy. I just need him.

Just Eden.

I reach for the button of my jeans, stopping to check with him first. "Is this okay?"

His eyes meet mine, and I can see the war within him. I can *feel* it. I can feel *all* of him inside of me. The flick of his wrists and featherlight steps he takes. His heartbeat that's now in sync with mine. Every blink, and every breath, they're no longer just his. Even his thoughts, the ones I despise. I can feel when they start to grow inside of him, consuming him from the inside out, because they consume me now, too. Everything about him does.

"I just want to lay down," I assure him. "Nothing else."

His brow creases with worry as I silently pray that he'll take this step. All I want is for him to leave his walls down for tonight. Just this once. He's given me so much, and I know that what I'm asking for is greedy, but I want it. I want it so fucking bad.

He's tense as he does it, but he gives me a single nod. My hands immediately move, slipping the metal button from the loop and pushing my pants to the floor in one swift movement. I'm in nothing but my black briefs, just like him, as I stride over and pull back the comforter. I hold it up in the air as I wait for him to crawl beneath the sheet. He stops in the middle of the bed and turns on his side to face me as I climb in behind him. His warmth is a beacon that my body follows, inching so close to him that our noses nearly touch. We're both breathing heavily, passing air back and forth between one another. I close my eyes, but I'm hyperaware of every part of my body. When he shifts and his leg brushes against mine. When his hand fists the blanket and pulls it closer to himself. When he rolls his head, trying to get his hair out of his face, and ends up even closer to me. I'm content to lay awake all night committing every move he makes to memory, but he seems restless.

I try to peek, to check on him, only to find his ocean eyes staring back at me. The dark blue edges nearly fade to white at the center, like seafoam on summer waves. He's *my* ocean. An ever-changing tide. Raging and at war one day, then calm and tranquil the next. Feral and unruly before fading into the predictable and contained.

"I love you..." he whispers remorsefully, cracking open a fissure in my chest. He's made little comments and remarks about his past, so I know that true affection wasn't something he had before he came here. It rips me open inside to think that this is probably the first time he's ever done anything like this with another person. That he spent his whole life being denied love to the point that he now feels guilty when he does. It makes me want to rampage, to storm the earth until I find the people that did this to him and put them six feet under. I could force them beneath the waves until their lungs filled with the salty ocean water. Taking their life with the wild nature of the very thing they tried to tame. That would feel symbolic. Even though it's something I would never actually do, *I think*, the idea brings a smile to my lips.

"I love you too, kid." I reply as I reach up and gently run my thumb across his jawline. My callused flesh brushes across his flawless skin. He's so soft. Inside and out.

"*Shhh...*" he chastises.

"No, Eden. *No.*" I prop up on my elbow to look down at him in frustration. "I won't whisper, because it's not a fucking secret. I will love you out loud. To anyone that asks. To everyone that doesn't. I'm not afraid to love you, because nothing about it is scary. It's beautiful. *You're* beautiful. What we have, it's so fucking beautiful that it's physically painful sometimes. I won't apologize to anyone else for the way I feel about you. Not now. Not *ever*. Okay? I won't."

His eyes bounce back and forth between mine as he digests what I've said silently. I'm not going to back down though. I need him to understand that these feelings are perfectly normal and that having them isn't a burden.

"Okay," he replies with a nod as he reaches out and touches my bottom lip with his finger. He's lost in thought as he runs it back and forth over the sensitive skin. I jolt forward, capturing his thumb between my teeth.

"*Ah*," he whimpers as his eyes meet mine. The shock fades away within seconds. His pupils start to dilate and fill with that same curious desire that I catch from him every now and then. As much as I want to feed into those desires, I told him that nothing was going to happen tonight, and I meant it. Our emotions are too high, and he's too vulnerable. Not to mention the fact that he's a fucking kid and I'm a grown ass man.

I open my jaw, letting his finger fall from my mouth, but his eyes stay locked onto mine. Usually, he realizes when he's looking at me like this and turns away in embarrassment. Not tonight, though. He's not backing down from his feelings for the first time since we met, and while I'm proud of him for doing that, it's dangerous. It's bold and reckless, and I like it *way* more than I should.

"If you play with fire, everything around you burns, Eden. You have to control it." I whisper reverently.

The same as always, he takes a second to process my words before speaking. His eyes pull away from mine as he rests his hand against my chest. My heart is racing, and I have no doubt that he can feel it thundering beneath his fingertips.

"I've never had control before, Dixon. That's why I— I don't think I know *how* to control it, and... I'm scared."

Scared of God.

Scared of hell. Scared of his parents. Scared of a religion that he's made it blatantly clear that he isn't even sure he believes in anymore.

"Here, let me help." I say as I lay back down. "Roll over."

He shuffles around until he's facing away from me. So, I wrap my arm around him and pull him against my chest. There's an immediate sense of relief, *of rightness*, in the way our bodies come together. I'm not sure if I'll ever have this again though, so I selfishly nuzzle closer, soaking up every ounce of him I can get.

"Have you ever been to the beach?" I ask.

"Once," he replies with a nod. "By myself."

"Did you touch the water?"

He nods again. I reach around, taking his hand into mine and holding it against his chest.

"When you stood at the edge of the shore, did you feel the way the waves start to steal the sand from beneath your feet?"

"Yeah," he replies as his thumb starts to rub against mine.

"And how did that make you feel?"

He's quiet for so long that I'm not sure if he's even going to answer me, but then his soft words finally come out. "Scared. Like I was going to fall."

"But if you keep standing there, keep enduring that feeling, it eventually dissipates. The sand stops moving, and you just get to enjoy the waves. It's like that. Sometimes getting through our own feelings is the hardest part. The rest of it, it's easy. *Simple.*"

"Nothing about *this*," he says as he raises our intertwined hands in the air. "Is simple, Dixon. *Nothing.*"

"Really?" I ask as I lean up to look at his face. "So, close your eyes for me."

He pinches them together, eager to do anything I request of him. "Alright. Imagine you're there. On the beach. You can feel the wind in your hair. The smell of the salty ocean right in front of you. Can you see it?"

He smiles as he nods at me. "I can hear the seagulls squawking on the pier."

I snicker, yet again amazed by this boy. "Good. Now you're gonna step into the water. Right at the edge of the waves. What happens, Eden?"

"It starts to do that. The sand starts to slide out from beneath my feet and it scares me." He admits as his brow furrows in concern. "It makes me want to take a step back. Out of the water."

"Did you step out of the water when you went to the beach on your own? Did you let the fear of the unknown ruin it for you?"

"Yes," he whispers as he nods. I can see a tear starting to squeeze out from between his lashes, so I lay back down and tug him closer to me. I close my eyes too, imagining that I'm there with him.

"This time..." I swallow the lump in my throat before I continue. "This time, you're standing in the water, and the sand starts to disappear from beneath your feet. You start to feel frightened, but something else happens."

"What? What happens?"

My heart races wildly in my chest as I let it play out in my mind. This is the first time I've let myself think about what Eden and I *could* look like. If things were different or we were in a different universe. If everything in the world was perfect, this is exactly what I'd want it to be like. *To feel like.*

"This time, I walk up behind you. I wrap my arms around your waist, and you lean against my chest. We're there. *Together.* Does that feel different?"

He's quiet, but I know that he's still awake because his grip on my hand tightens. Our combined breaths are the only thing echoing into the room, but it's almost as if I can actually hear the waves. Maybe that's just the sound of Eden.

"You don't have to be afraid now. I'm here." I whisper against the base of his neck, letting my lips drag across his flesh.

"I know," he replies. "I'm not scared anymore."

Me either.

Chapter Five

Dixon

I try to approach him quietly, but the gravel crunches beneath my feet, so I know he can hear me coming. He doesn't look back though. He keeps his eyes locked on the horizon like it holds all the secrets to the universe. Without even thinking, I glance down at the flimsy metal railing, the only thing keeping him on this side of heaven, before I look back up at him. Some days I actually believe this cliffside *does* have all the answers for him, but I wish it didn't.

"Hey kid," I say as I pull the pack of cigarettes from my pocket and lean against the hood.

"Hey, old man," he offers with a barely there smirk. He doesn't look in my direction though.

"Long day?" I ask as I scoot closer and pull him over for an awkward hug. He finally gives in, a real smile lighting up his face. I'm glad that I make him happy, but I wish that was enough for him.

"Not really," he replies as he shimmies his fingers at me until I pull out a cigarette for him, too. "I'm just nervous."

I let my arm rest on the hood behind him as I take a drag from my cigarette. "No reason to be nervous. Buster will love you. It's not like we've got any other mechanics in Willows. With Axel taking off, he needs the help."

"What if I mess it up?" He whispers before he digs his hand into my shirt pocket for the lighter.

"He's a cool dude. You're worrying too much."

He sighs before he sucks on his cigarette like it's his lifeline. He slides off the hood, just a foot or two from that stupid barrier that I love and hate in equal measures. I wish he'd never have come to this stupid park. I wish his heart didn't cling to it. I wish he didn't have this place as a back-up plan.

"I guess I better get going," he says as he jangles his keys around in his hand. "Don't wanna be late."

I pull him against my chest again, trying my best to share all the happiness I have with him. I hold him tighter, and probably a little longer than necessary.

"Alright, alright. I get it, old man." He says as he tries to shove me off of him. "I'll be alright."

I wish I believed him.

I guess I'm doing a whole lot of wishing these days.

I'm stirring a pot on the stove when the front door bangs against the wall before slamming closed. If I wasn't expecting him, I'd probably have shit myself. I can hear him struggling to get his shoes off in the entry way, too excited to slow down long enough to get them untied properly.

"Dixon!" He calls out. "Dixon!"

"In the kitchen!" I reply with a chuckle.

I hear him bouncing down the hall, and I can't help but smile. I knew Buster would love him. I knew from the moment I met him that he belonged here in Willows. *With me.* Hopefully he's starting to believe it, too.

He swings around the corner, the brightest smile I've ever seen on his face. "I got it!" He practically yells.

"I told you—" I start.

"I got it! I got it! I got it!" He belts out, interrupting me, as he starts dancing around the kitchen excitedly. I lean against the countertop, content to watch him like this for the rest of the night. His happiness leaks out, staining every nook and cranny of this house until it's the only thing that exists.

The same kitchen I've been standing in for over an hour, it's no longer the same. There are all these details, these things I overlooked, that seem important now. The lights are dim, music hums quietly in the background, and his shadow follows him around the island in cheerful circles. The sun is low in the sky, basking him in an orangey glow through the window, and I can finally start to smell the food I've been slaving over. It's taken me this long, too long, to realize that Eden doesn't just make my life better. He makes my life. *The entire damn thing.* He brings warmth and happiness, of course he does, but he also takes something that's been greyscale for longer than I can remember and paints it in every color of the rainbow.

He barrels into me, wrapping his arms around my waist. His eyes meet mine, and I think that maybe I was wrong earlier. I could stay like *this* for the rest of the night.

"I'm proud of you, kid." I say as I brush a stray strand of hair from his face. He blushes brightly before resting his head against my chest.

"I love you," he says quietly. It's no longer a whisper, so I can't complain.

"I love you too, Eden. Let's eat, yeah?"

He nods against my chest before pulling away.

His excitement sticks through dinner and well into the night. He crawls into my bed, where he's started spending every night, and curls against my side. He hums contentedly as he nuzzles against me until he's comfortable.

"How are you always so warm?" He asks affectionately.

I give him the only reply that comes to mind. "I was cold until I met you."

Chapter Six

EDEN

Buster is still taking a lot of time off, trying to spend the first couple of weeks helping his daughter with the baby as they get settled into their new lives. So, I only get to train two days a week right now. I don't mind it, really. I enjoy working with my hands, and it's a pretty good way to get back in the swing of things. Buster told me today that he thinks I'll be ready to start coming in full-time whenever he decides that he's ready to get back to working five days a week.

I'm so excited to tell Dixon that I can barely contain myself.

I bust through the front door, my shoes coming off just as fast as I can get the door closed behind me. I'm down the hall and swinging into the kitchen as I call out for him.

"Dix—" I start, swiftly choking on my words. "*Oh.*"

It takes a second for my brain to catch on to what's happening as I stare into the eyes of a frail little old lady puttering around Dixon's kitchen. She flicks the eye on the stovetop off and turns her full attention to me.

"Hi. Ma'am," I say with a nod. "I'm sorry. I didn't realize that—"

"You must be Eden," she interrupts with a sweet smile.

"Yes ma'am," I reply with a nod. "I didn't mean to barge in. I didn't know that Dixon had a guest."

"Oh stop," she says with a dismissive wave of her hand. "Please, call me Betty."

She rushes over, guiding me to a chair. I guess I'm sitting.

"I've just started dinner. Dixon is out working in the shop. He's told me all about you. I'm so excited to meet you."

Oh. "I'm surprised he's mentioned me," I reply as my cheeks heat in embarrassment.

"Don't be foolish, child. You practically live here, yes?" She asks as she walks back around to the oven.

"I... um, yes. I suppose I do. My house is just a few down the street. I'm renovating it right now."

I rub my hands together nervously as my eyes dart toward the back door. I really wish that Dixon would come inside. He should be expecting me. He's always expecting me.

"You like it here in Willows?" She asks as she opens the oven and checks on whatever she has cooking inside.

"Yes ma'am." I reply with a nod.

"You're very well mannered. Where did you come from?" She asks as the back door swings open. I've never been more grateful in my life. I really don't want to talk about this right now. Well, *not ever*, honestly.

"Ma," Dixon admonishes as he rounds the counter to wash his hands. He offers me an apologetic smile as he shakes his head. "I told you not to pester him with a bunch of questions."

She swings around, sassily placing a hand on her hip. "I am sixty-seven years old. I will damn well do as I please, Dixon." She says before pulling the dish rag from her shoulder and snapping it at him. He chuckles as he jumps to the side to avoid getting popped.

My brain is short-circuiting. I'm speechless as I watch them goofing off and cutting up with one another. He pulls the little old lady between his strong arms and hugs her just as tenderly as he does with me, leaving a little peck atop her head.

I wonder if this is what parents are supposed to be like with their children. I can feel the love between them like it's a tangible thing that I can reach out and touch. If I were just a little bit closer, I think I might could. I'd stretch out with my fingertips, and it'd start to seep into my soul, filling all the empty places my parents left behind. I shouldn't though. It isn't meant for me.

I push my chair back, clearing my throat as I force myself to my feet. "I should go. I have plenty of things I could be doing. I'll let you two—"

"Don't be silly, kid." Dixon says as he grabs my wrist and pulls me to his chest. "You're staying. Ma already made dinner for us."

My body goes rigid against his, and it's so out of the ordinary for us, so wrong, that it fills me with disgust. The way Dixon and I are together, I would never act that way in front of my parents. I can feel their judgement piercing my skin even with the hundreds, possibly thousands, of miles between us. My eyes dart to his mother nervously, but she just smiles in our direction. I can feel acceptance and pure admiration shining through her gaze, and it gives me the permission I need to melt against his chest the way I normally would.

"How was your day?"

I glance up at him, my excitement returning. "Buster said when he goes back to work full-time, he thinks I'll be ready to dive right in with him." I explain, my eyes locked with his.

His smile says everything I need it to. That he's excited for me. That he knew I could do this. That he'll be with me every step of the way. *Always.*

"I'm proud of you, Eden." He says with adoration, warming my chest.

I blush, glancing over to his mother.

"I guess it's a good thing I made an apple pie. This is clearly something to celebrate, yes?" She asks curiously.

"Yes ma'am—"

"Betty," she chides with a scowl.

"Betty," I correct with a chuckle as I pull away from Dixon. "That sounds lovely."

"Good," she says with a nod as she slings the dish rag over her shoulder. "Now sit. It's time to eat, son."

Dixon leads me to the table in the dining area today, instead of the island, despite the fact that it's only a few steps away. His mother brings over platters of food, declining any help we offer. She's happy to hear us chatter about our lives, our jobs, our day-to-day activities, but the moment anything about her life is mentioned, she cages up. As the night goes on, I get a feeling that there's a reason she's avoiding talking about her life back home, and Dixon is clearly picking up on the same hints of deflection.

"Ma," he finally says before taking a drink of water. "How is dad doing?"

It doesn't filter in slowly, the tension in the room stifles within seconds. I couldn't paddle through it with a rowboat. That's for damn sure. She clears her throat as she takes the cloth napkin from her lap and wipes her mouth.

"As you'd expect," she answers dryly as she forces her chair out from beneath the table.

"Ma," Dixon begs. "How is he actually doing?"

She gathers her plate, content to busy herself cleaning it off in the sink.

"You should visit him."

"You know I can't do that, Ma." He says remorsefully.

"He doesn't have much time left, Dixon. It's time the two of you got over this— this... whatever it is."

"He chose this. You know he wants me there as much as I want to be there. It wouldn't do anything but make it worse."

She drops the dishes in the sink, water splashing all over the counter, and clattering loudly as she slaps the faucet off. I startle at the commotion, my instincts flaring to life. The hairs all over my body prickle as they stand on end. I freeze, my spine going stiff as I turn my attention to Dixon. His eyes are firmly planted on his mother, and when I look to her, she's staring right back at him.

"This is ridiculous, Dixon. He's going to die and the last memory you'll have of him will be—" She pauses, wiping at the tears forming in her eyes. "Will be something foolish and you're both going to regret it."

"He won't regret anything, Ma. He'll be dead." He replies sadly.

"Dixon," she barks angrily as she tugs the rag from her shoulder and slaps it down on the counter.

"I'm not going, Ma. That's all there is to it." Dixon says firmly as he pushes out his own chair. His eyes finally meet mine, and I can feel all the apologies pouring out of him. I know he didn't plan for this to happen, but that doesn't make it any less uncomfortable to witness. I look down at my lap, hoping that I can manage to make myself disappear until this is over.

I nearly jump out of my skin when a frail little hand lands on my shoulder. When I look up at her, the exact same green and gold eyes that Dixon has stare back at me. Even with the current circumstances, I can feel the depth of her kindness, and somehow, I just know that she's responsible for Dixon being the man he is. I want to thank her, to explain to her, what kind of man she raised. Everything he does for me. *What he means to me.* Perhaps this isn't the best time though, so I stay quiet.

Her cold hand comes to my chin, nothing but adoration shining back at me despite the animosity that was spit across the room just moments ago.

"You're a lovely boy," she says with pride that makes my heart stutter in my chest. "He's lucky to have found you, Eden."

"Thank you, m— Betty." I whisper back.

She smiles sweetly before releasing me and disappearing down the hallway. I stare down at my empty plate as I listen to her grab her things. Her heels, that I somehow didn't even notice when I came in, echo against the floor as she slips them on. Her keys jingle loudly as she pulls them from her bag. The door creaks in a way I've never noticed before as she quietly opens it and sees herself out. All the sounds echo on repeat in my brain, leaving a heaviness that I'm far too familiar with.

Dixon pulls my chair from beneath the table, picks me up, and carries me to bed.

When I wake up in the morning, Dixon is out in the shop. The house is eerily silent as I sneak my way through the dark hall. I round the corner, nearly stumbling in shock. The kitchen is *spotless*. All the food we left at the table last night, it's gone. The dishes are already cleaned and put away. The counters have been wiped down. The trash can is empty.

I wander over to the oven, opening it to see if the pie that was left to stay warm still remains, but it too has succumbed to Dixon's purge. No sign of his mother's presence from just hours ago remains, and it's clear to me that this is how he deals with the demons of his past. Whatever happened between him and his father, he wants no reminders of it. So much so, that he doesn't even want to remember that his mother was in his space.

I decide not to bring it up. Ever.

Even though I really wanted some of that pie.

Chapter Seven

EDEN

I pull out the rag from my back pocket as I stand up. I glance around at the shop as I wipe the grease from my hands. Buster's place is older, but that adds a bit of charm to it, I think. The layers of dust and fingerprints on all the surfaces don't make it seem dirty, they just make it feel used. *Loved.*

I glance down at my hands. Grease and grime are caked beneath my nails and stain the lines that run along every crease. It's familiar. Almost nostalgic.

Using my hands feels good. I hadn't realized how much I'd missed this.

Evan, one of Buster's many children, strolls up beside me as he takes a big swig of water from a bottle. He lets out a thirsty sigh as he glances over the brakes I just replaced. "That looks great. You work pretty quick to be so young."

My eyes follow the bobbing of his Adam's apple as he swallows another drink. Sweat trickles down his sun-tanned skin alongside a beautifully prominent vein. He reminds me of another beautiful man that's been invading my *private* thoughts lately.

Evan and I have become pretty good friends the last few weeks. He's a pretty chill guy. We cut up and have a good time while we're working, and that makes the days fly by.

I tear my eyes away from him, glancing down at my work. "It's all I've ever known. Machines just come naturally to me."

Half-truth.

Mechanic work does come easily to me... now. It didn't always, though. This is the kind of work my parents intended for me to do for the rest of my life. It was supposed to be my contribution to their little community. At seven years old, instead of playing with my friends after school, I was carted off to the mechanic's shop. The frail old man almost gave up on teaching me, because nothing would click. The pistons, the spark plugs, chips, radiators, hoses, dielectric grease, my little brain couldn't compute it all. I couldn't grasp it, until I just... did.

One day, he pulled me aside. "Listen son, you *have* to get this. Think of it as a community, *a village*. Each part relies on another part to do it's job. I need people to use their vehicles in order for me to have work. They rely on me, but I rely on them just as much. Cars are the same way."

"Like symbiosis?"

"Like who?"

"Nothing," I murmur. "Show me again. I'll get it. I swear." I replied with a sigh of resignation.

He gave me a sad smile, but nodded in agreement.

I think about him often. I feel bad for wasting so much of his time. He had to be ready to retire, but I'm sure they've made him stay to train someone else. He wouldn't really have any other option unless he chose to leave like I did. It wouldn't have been too much of a burden, really. He never had a partner, was never married, like many of the men there. Only certain men got that privilege.

My father was *the father*. He spoke with the Lord. *Supposedly*. He was the one who chose what men were 'gifted' wives from God.

Gossip happens everywhere you go, so the whispers were unavoidable. A comment here, a remark there, and it didn't take long for me to start piecing together the reality of the situation. The nights my father didn't come home, the meetings only for grown-ups, the pairing off of certain boys and girls at young ages. When I turned sixteen, my father sat me down and told me that God had decided that I wouldn't have a wife. I was kind of relieved, honestly. I didn't find any of the girls there interesting. They were all so bland, so... conforming. They all looked the same, acted the same, did all the same things.

The relief wore off quickly though. Why didn't God think I was deserving? Was it because I struggled to learn the things he wanted me to do? Was it because I didn't find the girls attractive? That couldn't be the answer though, right? Because if God made me in his image then he would think I was perfect, right?

That's when I really started questioning things. I started paying attention. *Listening*.

The reason I could never have a wife? It had nothing to do with God. It was because all the girls around my age... they were my sisters. Well, *half-sisters*. My father held reproductive rights to every single woman, even other men's wives, like they were all cattle. My father's best friend, he was the only other man that wasn't forced to get a vasectomy, and he didn't have any daughters close to my age.

After I figured that out, it didn't take long for me to start noticing other things. The way my father would devour girls with his eyes when they'd walk into a room. How he'd pull them aside and disappear with them for hours. How the girls would return in one of two ways. Preening from what I imagine was my father promising them God's favor for the things he'd coax them into doing, or they'd return defeated and ashamed. I saw the way certain girls avoided him. They would go out of their way to put as much distance between them and my father as they could, to the point of isolating themselves. I don't understand why they did it, why any of them believed that hogwash.

I'm sure my mother felt like a queen. She had the man that ruled the roost, but at what cost? Sleeping alone most nights while your husband warmed the bed of girls younger than some of his own children? Popping out kids like a prized breeding heifer just to know that all the boys would likely be cursed to a life of loneliness while the girls... as soon as they were adults, they were already promised to a man that was triple their age. Or more. It was disgusting. All of it.

Leaving was a no-brainer. Finding the opportunity to do it, *that* took a little more planning

"How long you been doing this?" He asks as he squats down to look over my work like brakes aren't one of the easiest things to do.

"A long time," I reply as I tuck the rag back into my pocket. "Since I was seven."

"I can tell," he replies as he stands up and faces me. "You're good."

Evan isn't much older than me. Maybe in his mid-twenties. There's no wedding band on his hand. I've been working here a few weeks, and he hasn't mentioned having a girlfriend either. Sometimes I catch him watching me in a way that makes my insides swirl uncomfortably.

When my eyes catch his, my cheeks heat. "Thanks."

"It's nice to have a competent set of hands to help out around here," he slaps my shoulder proudly as he starts to walk off. "I'm happy to have you around."

"You're not alone in that regard," a voice I'd recognize anywhere chimes in. "Willows wouldn't be the same without him. Would it, Evan?"

Evan turns back, sharing a silent exchange with Dixon. The tension in the room thickens, creating a heavy fog that seems misplaced.

"He was just complimenting my work, Dixon." I explain.

"I bet he was," he replies with his eyes still on Evan before finally turning to me. "You're good at what you do."

Finally, *finally*, he graces me with that smile that's warmer than the sun. My cup that was half empty, his presence fills it until it starts to overflow. When he turns his attention back to Evan, I feel a tickle deep in my chest that I don't know how to scratch. I don't like his eyes on Evan. I want them on me.

I take off in a sprint, hopping on his back. He chuckles as I use my feet to climb up him like the apple trees I spent my summers stealing snacks from. When I finally manage to get high enough to lean over his shoulder and stare at him, he reaches up and ruffles my sweaty hair lovingly.

That's better.

"Hey, kid." He whispers as he leans his forehead against mine.

"Hey, old man." I reply with a smile that gives away exactly how happy I am.

Evan hums thoughtfully, causing us both to turn in his direction. His brow rises curiously as he watches the two of us.

"I think I understand," he says with a nod as he pulls a rag from his pocket. "We've finished everything on the schedule. Why don't you go ahead and call it a day, Eden?"

I turn to Dixon excitedly, "Yay! Let's go do something fun!" I exclaim as I drop from his back.

He chuckles as he turns to face me. "How about we go to the diner instead? Grab a bite to eat?"

"Oh! Yes! A milkshake sounds perfect!" I say as I grab my phone from the top of the toolbox and toss my dirty rag in its place.

"And a burger, Eden. You have to eat real food too, kid."

"Yeah, yeah." I groan miserably. "*And a burger*. Oh, with some onion rings!"

I weave my arm between his and tug him toward the open bay door. When I look up at him though, his attention is on Evan. Again.

An uneasiness washes over me as I turn to look at him, too. A smirk that reminds me of my father is on his lips, and his eyes devour Dixon and I unabashedly. It's all devious and dreadful. It's like a freezing cold bucket of water has been thrown on me. I'm drenched in memories of the way my father made a game out of using and abusing people. He did nothing but make a mockery of people and their naivety. If Evan thinks that he's about to start toying with Dixon and I, he has another thing coming. My mood shifts instantly, my hackles rising.

"No," I say as I point to Dixon. "He is mine. And I'm his." I say sternly.

Dixon glances down at me with pride, his eyes softening.

I turn my eyes back to Evan, glaring at him. "I mean it, Evan."

He throws his hands up defensively, "Loud and clear. Y'all have a good evening, yeah?"

I nod, keeping my eyes on him as I shove Dixon toward the door.

"What was that about?" He whispers as we step outside.

"He had that look," I reply with annoyance. "It reminded me of my father."

"Ah," he hums. "Because he was flirting."

My eyes dart to him, my skin crawling in a way that makes me want to gag. "You don't know that."

"I know him well enough to know that he most definitely was, Eden. Have you ever seen him act that way with women?"

I filter through my memories from the last few weeks we've worked together. I'm struggling to place any instances of him talking to women, but I'm not finding anything. *At all.* Every time a woman walks through the door, he lets me or Buster help them.

"That doesn't mean anything," I deflect as I yank open the passenger door and climb inside.

"Whatever you say, kid." Dixon chuckles condescendingly as he shakes his head.

I hate when he does this. He acts like I don't know anything just because I'm younger than him. I'm aware that I was sheltered and there's still a lot of things I haven't experienced, but I'm learning. I've been on my own for years now.

"Quit calling me that," I demand as he wiggles the key into the ignition. "I don't like it when you treat me like I'm stupid just because you're older than I am. Age doesn't equate to knowledge."

He glares over at me in shock. "Wha— Why—" He stutters out. "This has nothing to do with your age, Eden. That's irrelevant. You're brilliant, no matter how young you are."

"Then why are you acting like I have no idea what I'm talking about?"

"Eden," he sighs. "It's because Evan and I... we're both gay."

"*Oh...*"

"Yeah. So maybe just trust me on this one." He says with confidence as he cranks the truck.

"He told you that?"

"He didn't have to. Half the town told me before we'd even met."

"Okay," I resign as I shift in my seat. "Well, how do I make him *not* do that?"

He turns out of the parking lot, chuckling before briefly glancing over at me. "I think you handled it, Eden."

"Good," I say proudly. "Now, about that burger. Is that nonnegotiable?"

"Yep."

"*Fuck.*"

Chapter Eight

EDEN

"Wow," I mutter under my breath.

I click another link, my eyebrows rising in shock. I watch the computer screen, certain that I'm hallucinating.

"There's no way that's fitting in there. *No. Way.*" I argue with myself.

It most definitely *did* fit. Among many other completely asinine things that most definitely do not belong in any orifice of the body. Especially not that one.

I may be young, but I'm not completely stupid. My body isn't waiting around for my brain to get on board. If I get another hard-on while cuddling with Dixon, I might literally die of embarrassment. He brushes it off every time, but this is getting out of hand. I had to take matters into my own hands. *Literally.*

What was supposed to be a jerk-off session while Dixon was at work turned into a very enlightening trip down a black hole.

One thing became clear *very* quickly.

I'm not into girls.

At all. Not even a little bit.

Did you know there's videos of them with dogs and horses and— Never mind. Note to self: Stay off the internet.

The sun is settling in the sky, streaming through the window and splintering across the room. The front door creaks open, and I'm so excited Dixon's home that I forget what I was doing. As his socked feet start padding down the hallway, I finally realize that I'm sitting half-naked at his dining-room table. I panic, scrambling to close the browser, and barely managing to slam the laptop closed only seconds before he enters the kitchen.

His eyes scan over me only briefly, as if this is a perfectly normal occurrence, before he throws his lunchbox on the counter and starts unpacking it. His eyes cut to me again, causing him to chuckle.

"Are you waiting on me to point out the obvious, Eden?"

"Maybe..."

"You were jerking off." It's a statement.

"No," I reply with a scowl as I fold my arms across my bare chest. It's only a half-truth. I *wasn't* jerking off, but I had initially planned to.

"Sure," he replies with another laugh.

Dick.

"I wasn't," I say sternly as I gesture to my crotch. "Look."

He looks. *Boy, does he look.* Which doesn't help my argument at all, because I immediately start growing under his attention. He laughs again as he turns away, which just irritates me.

"Fine," I say as I shove my chair back and stomp up the stairs.

I slam the bathroom door closed and turn on the shower. I know what it looked like, but I don't understand why he doesn't believe me. It's aggravating. He never fucking listens to me.

Only seconds after I've stripped my boxers and slid beneath the warm water, the bathroom door creaks open.

"Go away," I demand as I stick my head beneath the water.

He doesn't reply, but when I open my eyes, he's already in the shower with me.

"I said go away," I clarify.

"This is my shower, kid." He replies nonchalantly as he steps around me to wet his hair.

I huff as I step to the side, giving him the warm water. I should've just gone home.

"I do it all the time, Eden. It's nothing to be embarrassed about."

"I'm not embarrassed!" I reply as I throw my hands up in exasperation. "Because I wasn't jerking off!"

He eyes me suspiciously, clearly not convinced. "Alright. Fine. I'll bite. What were you doing, then?"

My cheeks heat, shame flooding my body. I clear my throat nervously. "Um… well, that was my original plan."

"But?"

"But I couldn't."

"You *couldn't*? Why not?"

"It...uh, it wouldn't work."

He hums thoughtfully as he steps back around me. I slink beneath the water, letting it wash away some of these nasty feelings. He moves closer to me, his hands finding my hips. His closeness is a shock to my system. My skin prickles and my spine tingles. I'm high on the way his touch brings my body to life.

I sigh out a relaxed groan as I let my body lean into his. This feeling, it's worth dying for.

As his body presses against mine, his hands move to my stomach. My chest. My throat. He's everywhere and nowhere at the same time. His touch and the smell of him are the only things I can even sense anymore. After a long day at the park, he smells like pine trees and the ocean breeze. It's perfectly him, and I love it.

Because I love him, I think to myself, but I don't know if that's true, so I ignore it.

He guides our bodies until he's propped against the shower wall. His hands are still trailing across my flesh, weaving intricate webs of desire I fear I'll never untangle.

His fingers lace between the strands of my hair, tightening as he gently tilts my head to the side.

"It looks like it's working just fine, Eden." He whispers against my neck. My dick is harder than it's ever been, so I really didn't need him to tell me that. I just need him to keep touching me.

"Dixon," I whine, begging for something. What I'm begging for, I'm not sure

"Touch it," he whispers before digging his teeth into my flesh. I instinctively try to pull away from him, but before either of us have time to blink, I'm right back against him like a cat in heat. He's hard against my back. So fucking hard.

I reach down, tugging at my balls a couple times before I give in and stroke myself. This is going to end embarrassingly quickly.

The pleasure is blinding, the most intense thing I've ever felt, but it isn't what I actually want.

He still has one hand tangled in my hair, but I search for the other, slipping my fingers between his to guide him lower.

"Eden," he warns with desperation.

"Please," I beg. "*Please.*"

His teeth sink into my flesh again, but I'm too distracted to recoil from the pain. He quickly replaces it anyway, licking away the sting before sucking at my skin until it's most definitely left a bloodstained reminder in the shape of his lips.

His fingers stay intertwined with mine until we're both stroking them on my cock in tandem. He groans as he ruts against my back. I swear to God, I've died. This has to be heaven.

I move my hand, giving him full control, as I melt into his body.

"Is this what you need, Eden? Someone to take care of you?" He asks as his hand works me over.

"*Fuck*. Yes," I hiss. "I'm so close."

"Are you gonna watch me when you're done? I need you to see what you do to me, kid."

I nod enthusiastically. "Oh God," I gasp as an explosion of pleasure rips from my body. It's overwhelming, and I'm in a hazy afterglow as Dixon forces his way from behind me. I'm panting out heavy labored breaths as he faces me and uses one arm to prop himself against the shower wall. He locks his eyes with mine, never tearing them away.

"This is how much I've wanted you, Eden." He whispers. "I shouldn't. I know I shouldn't, but... *fuck*."

"I'm yours," I reply earnestly. *Always.*

When he's done and marked my body as his, he rests his forehead against mine. I smile. My heart is so full of happiness and love that it's overflowing. I could stay here with him forever. I never want this moment to end.

Until I do.

"I'm sorry, Eden." He says as he brushes a thumb across my cheek tenderly. "I shouldn't have done that."

I don't want him to see the way tears are welling up in my eyes, or how my lips start quivering, so I turn away from him.

I'm not sorry.

Chapter Nine

EDEN

When it's dark, in my head, it's *really* dark.

I've researched it a lot. Too much, honestly. That word that no one likes to talk about. *Depression.*

I know that the symptoms are different for everyone. I know that *my* symptoms, they're normal. Common, even. That doesn't mean that they feel like it. That doesn't mean that I feel any better about them when they show up. It doesn't mean that I can manage them any better. It doesn't even mean that I feel a fraction less alone than I would've before I knew. It's still the same shitty ride I was on before, just with a little less confusion.

I don't have good thoughts on my bad days. Granted there aren't a lot of bad thoughts, either. In fact, I barely have any thoughts at all. I'm not a glass half full or a glass half empty. I'm just... *empty*.

It's like I'm not even real. I'm just taking up space that someone else, *someone more deserving*, could use. I'm not a good friend. I'm not a good employee. I'm not a good person. So, I do my best to disappear in the only way I can. Into myself.

I pick at a blade of grass between my fingers, wishing that it felt more like... something. Anything, really. I stare up at the sky, into the never-ending spin of the universe. The clouds, the stars, the moon. All the things that usually makes me feel grateful to be here? Tonight they just make me feel nothing. They don't add or take away from the emptiness I feel in my chest. They just exist in the same universe, uneventfully.

I blink a couple of times, trying to get the tears that are welling up in my eyes to fall away so that I can see them a little clearer. *Still nothing*. I've been laying here since the sun was still in the sky, hours and hours. I've never been so alone, or at least, that's how it feels. It doesn't matter that last night I was laughing and cuddling with Dixon on his couch. That was yesterday. That was *before*.

With the sun having disappeared not that long ago, I know that he'll come looking for me soon. He's already on his way, I'm sure. I should be happy that I won't be alone anymore, grateful even, but I'm not. I just feel guilty that he's going to find me like this. *Again*. That he's going to come over here after working all day just to take care of me. He never complains, and I'm so appreciative of that. Truly. I can always see the hurt in his eyes though and that... it makes me feel like shit.

"Eden!"

I wince as I roll onto my side. *I knew it.* I knew he was coming. I can practically feel him in my soul. The bond we have with one another is unlike anything I've ever felt before, and all I can do is hope and pray that he doesn't tap into my feelings the way I tap into his. I don't think I could deal with the knowledge that I make him feel this way. I could never forgive myself.

I can sense his energy, his sunshine, as it gets closer. My body isn't absorbing it the way it normally does, but I can still feel it radiating off of him. Until it stops.

"Eden Arbor," he growls as he rushes to my side. "Why didn't you answer the phone, kid?"

I shrug as I pick at more blades of grass. "Don't know where it's at."

"Jesus," he huffs. "Come on."

He bends down to pick me up, and I have a moment of sheer panic. Of devastating loss. Then I realize that I can just break off the pieces of grass and take them with me as I'm lifted in the air. I grab a handful, nearly ripping the roots from the ground. Dixon glances down at me as I grasp them tightly against my chest. He doesn't say it's silly. He doesn't chastise me. He doesn't judge me. He just takes every part of me and cherishes them more than anything else in the universe. The ugly, the irrational, the unreasonable. He takes it all. Happily. I can't even fathom how he could see me this way and still think that I'm worth all this trouble. I can't help but wonder if that's what love is actually supposed to be like.

"Do you regret what we did?" I whisper.

"No," he says before pausing. "I should, but I don't."

We're both quiet as he carries me through the gate and down the sidewalk until we're at his house. He never asks me what I want to do. He refuses to let me walk through the darkness alone. He says he's here to be my lighthouse, to guide me back home. I think that maybe, *just maybe*, he actually does.

"Do you love me, Dixon?" I ask as I look up at him. He glances down at me, his eyes softening. He doesn't seem to be bothered by my swollen, damp eyes, or that I'm wearing the same clothes I was in yesterday.

"Of course, I do, kid. You know I do." He says as he pushes his bedroom door open and strolls inside.

"No," I say as I pinch off the blade of grass between my fingers and pull it apart at the center to distract myself. "I mean… do you *love* me."

He's quiet as he takes the handful of grass from my fist and puts them on the nightstand. He carries me to the bathroom and flicks on the shower. He moves around the space methodically, with purpose, spinning around to drop me on the countertop before he strips off his shirt and jeans, leaving him in nothing but his boxers. I've seen him like this a hundred times now, and it never gets old. In fact, it's gotten *less* old every time. My eyes linger a little longer every time, and I don't know what it means that I don't want to tear my eyes away from him. That I want to reach out and trace every inch of his body like the work of art it is.

His eyes catch mine before he reaches out for the hem of my hoodie. I raise my arms to allow him to pull it over my head. I slide off the counter and start unbuttoning my pants myself. He would've done it if I didn't, but there are weird things happening right now that I don't want him to notice yet. After what happened the other night, how he acted afterward, I'm reluctant to be back in his shower at all. Especially *with* him. Just being in this bathroom is a visual reminder that has my body responding.

It doesn't seem like I'm going to be able to hide it for long though, because he reaches down for his boxers and gives me a questioning glare. What am I supposed to say? That he can't shower naked in his own damn house? Obviously not. I swallow nervously as I nod but still turn to the side to give him some privacy. The shower door opens, but as I peek over my shoulder, I can still see him in my peripheral.

"Are you going to get in, Eden?"

I clear my throat as I shift on my feet. "Are you going to answer my question?"

"If you get in the shower and let me wash you off."

I glance down at myself and curse my body. There's no way this thing is going away, and we both know that he isn't going to let me crawl in that bed until I'm clean. I'm sure that if I said I was uncomfortable, that he'd let me shower alone, but I'm tired of being alone. We've slept in the bed together dozens of times at this point, and I know he's seen it before, but that doesn't make me any less embarrassed about it. I chew on the inside of my cheek as I debate what I want to do.

"Fine," I huff out as I rip off my boxers before I can change my mind. I close my eyes and take a deep breath before getting the courage to turn around. His eyes don't even wander, he keeps them locked with mine as he reaches out for me. I take his hand in mine and let him lead me into the shower. The warm water slices through the heaviness, washing away some of the burdens I've been carrying on my shoulders all day.

He directs me under the water first, lifting my chin so that he can soak my hair. I let my eyes flutter closed as his fingers massage my scalp. His touch is pure magic as it works tension from miles below the surface of my skin.

"Would that scare you?" He whispers.

"Not today," I answer honestly. "I'm just trying to... *learn*."

"Learn what, exactly?"

"If that's the feeling in my chest."

"Even if I love *you*, it doesn't mean that you love *me*, Eden. Or that you ever will, and I know that. I knew it from the beginning, and I'm okay with that."

"But you *do* love me?" I ask as I open my eyes and look up at him. His movements stop, only for a second, as his gaze catches mine.

"Yeah," he replies as he turns away to grab the shampoo. "I do."

"When?"

He chuckles as he squirts soap into his palm. "What do you mean when?"

"I mean *when*? How long?"

His brow furrows as he reaches up and starts scrubbing my head. His eyes meet mine as he continues to wash my hair. "It doesn't really work like that. Not for me, anyway."

He guides my chin back until the bubbles start sliding down my body. He turns his attention back to what he's doing, careful not to let soap get in my face.

"It just kind of... *happened*. Over time."

"How do you know that's what it is?" I ask as he grabs the loofa and lathers soap on it.

He waves his finger around in the air, demanding I turn around. He starts scrubbing my back before moving down to my legs. I pick at my fingernails nervously, unable to enjoy the way he's pampering me, as I wait on his answer.

"Because you're the most important thing to me." He finally replies. I glance over my shoulder at him as I think about it. He stares back at me, patiently awaiting whatever I have to say. The truth is there. Plain as day. It isn't rocket science.

"You're the most important thing to me, too."

He abruptly tears his eyes away from me. "No, I'm not, Eden."

After he finishes, he grabs my shoulders and forces me to spin back around. He scrubs over my chest and arms before handing the loofa over to me to finish the rest. He busies himself with washing his own body, but there's a stifling silence that hangs between us.

When the water is off, and we're wrapped in fluffy towels, I scrounge up the bravery to speak aloud the only thing my brain can think.

"I don't understand, Dixon."

"I know, kid. It's okay." He says as he hangs up his towel and slides on his underwear. I try to keep my eyes away, but it's hard. It's so hard to listen to my head when my body wants something else. And I do. I want him so bad that the desire I have to just reach out and touch him has my insides quivering.

"There are things that are more important to you, Eden. I know you care about me, and that's what's important, okay? That's what matters to me."

"But you *are* the most important thing to me, Dixon."

He gives me a weak smile before turning away to push the door open. "Come on, kid. Let's get in bed."

As soon as we step into the bedroom, the blades of grass stare back at me from the nightstand. I feel irrationally irritated by their presence, or rather the *reason* for their presence. I slide open the window beside the bed and snatch them off the nightstand. I chunk them out the window and dust off my hands confidently before shoving it closed again. When I turn back around, Dixon is watching me with a proud smirk on his face.

Today wasn't perfect, but as I crawl beneath the sheets beside him, I still consider it a win.

Chapter Ten

Dixon

Wood shavings cover my hands. And the table, and the sander, and pretty much *everything* within a ten-foot radius. Between work, helping Eden empty all the trash from the house, and building the pantry, it's taken me a while to get all the cabinet doors just how I wanted them. I step back to admire my work at the exact same time that Eden pounces on my back.

"Hey, kid." I chuckle as I grab ahold of his arm to help him hang on. "What are you getting into today?"

"I just spent the last hour making a mess in your kitchen. Here," he says as he shoves a cookie toward my face. "They're *delicious*."

"When are you gonna start destroying your own kitchen instead of mine," I ask as I stare down at the cookie.

"When are you going to finish my cabinets so that I have a kitchen to use? Hm?"

Touche'.

Once I'm satisfied that there are no raisins in the cookie he's thrusting in my face, I lean over and take a bite from his hand.

"Jesus, kid." I scoff as the gooey chocolatey concoction melts in my mouth. "Where did you learn to cook like this?"

"I have lots of sisters," he says with a shrug.

"Why am I always making dinner then?" I mumble with a mouth full of cookie.

He shrugs bashfully. "I can bake better than I can cook. And I like when you cook for me," he replies as he drops from my back.

As I lean down to dust off my pants, Eden wanders over to the table, brushing his fingers along the cabinet door I just finished. He's probably seen them a dozen times since I started working on them, but he seems just as enamored today as he did the first time he saw them.

"I love them," he says as he looks up at me.

"The cabinets? Or your sisters?" I joke.

His brow furrows in confusion. "The cabinets, Dixon." He replies as he points to them.

"How many sisters do you have?" I ask as I step up behind him and tug him against my chest. He rests his head against me and looks up as he shrugs.

"At least a dozen. Maybe more."

I know I've made comments about him being from a cult before, but guilt hits me for it a little late. It's clear that even if he doesn't call it that, even if he doesn't see it as clearly as I do, a cult is exactly what it was.

"I'm sorry," I offer as I wrap my arms around him.

"There's nothing to be sorry for, Dixon." He says as he glances toward the door. "I'm happy now."

I think about how Eden said he's bounced around, fixed up houses, and left, and I wonder if that's what he plans to continue doing. I try really hard not to think about it, because I don't know how I feel about him leaving in the near future. I honestly don't know how I could ever go back to the way my life was without him.

"You like it in Willows?" I ask as I prop my head on top of his.

"Of course, I do."

"Do you— Are you planning to leave? When you finish the house?"

"When I got here, I was."

"And now?" I ask, despite not being sure if I want the answer.

"Nah," he says as he shakes his head. "These cabinets look too good. I think I'd miss them."

I can't help but smile before leaning down to kiss the top of his head.

Weeks after Eden mentioned it, we finally went to the furniture store and brought home a new bed. I'm not sure if he was saving up money for it, or if he liked staying at my place so much that it slipped his mind, but it's a bittersweet feeling. I'm proud of him, but... I don't know if his ghost in my bed will be good enough anymore.

I look over at him before rolling on my side and propping myself up on my elbow. "Does this mean you're gonna stop sleeping at my place now?"

His brow furrows as he turns toward me. He grabs my other hand and tugs on it until I'm leaning over him.

"In your dreams," he whispers. "It just means that you're going to be sleeping here with me sometimes."

I chuckle. "Is that right, kid?"

"Mhm," he hums happily as his eyes lock with mine.

Sometimes it's easy to forget how young he is, but not tonight. He practically shines, so much hope and happiness staring back at me. Where I have wrinkles starting to form around my eyes, he's soft and untouched by time. I brush my thumb along the corner of his mouth, where I hope there will be laugh lines in the future instead of lines from frowning. Honestly, I just hope he makes it far enough to see them in the mirror, because I doubt I'll still be around to witness it.

Not that I don't want to be, because I do, but he's still a kid. He'll move on. He'll get tired of me. He'll wake up one day and realize that he should be with someone his own age, and I'll stay here. Still living in Willows. Still living with his ghost, because even when he's long gone, he'll always be it for me.

"Kiss me," he whispers as he stares up at me.

"Eden..." I start, but he shoves a finger over my lips to silence me.

"Don't you dare take this moment from me. I don't want a lecture. I don't want an apology. I don't want to hear how much we shouldn't do it. I want a kiss, Dixon. And come hell or high water, I'm getting it."

I smirk as I reach up to move his finger from my mouth. I lean down, and press my lips to his, and just as I expected, it's not enough. When I roll to my back, he follows, his lips never leaving mine as he straddles my waist. That doesn't really feel like enough either...

But when it comes to Eden, I'm not sure I could *ever* get enough.

Chapter Eleven

EDEN

I had a long day. A *really* long day. Everything went wrong, and I was covered in oil from head to toe. I decided to shower at my house instead of tracking it all over Dixon's house, but now I'm getting here late and he's probably wondering where the hell I've been. I pause at the front door and consider knocking since I'm so late, but he'd probably just laugh at me, so I push my way inside.

"Dixon," I call out as I slip off my shoes.

"In here, kid." He replies from his room. I follow the sound of his voice, surprised to find him all dressed up. He's wearing a nice pair of jeans and a button up flannel shirt with a big jacket like the one I wear to work. His hair is damp and combed back. The silver hairs at his temples are striking. He looks handsome. *Really handsome.*

"I... uh, I have something I need to take care of."

My eyes meet his as my brows pinch together in confusion. Is he saying that he has something he needs to do without me? We do everything together. *Everything.*

"Can I come?"

"Well, you can, but it's not going to be much fun, kid."

I shake my head in denial. "I don't care."

"Alright," he says as he grabs his keys and wallet from atop his dresser that's become more of *our* dresser. In fact, I think he only uses the top two drawers. The other three are stuffed full of my belongings. "Let's get going then."

I climb into his truck, barely able to sit still with anticipation. Based on the way Dixon is dressed, and how standoffish he's being, I suspect he may have been telling the truth. This isn't going to be fun.

Whatever this is, it seems important to him, and that means it's important to me.

When we drive two towns over and he pulls into the parking lot of a giant stone cathedral, I decide that he was probably right. I should've just stayed home.

Why do I have to be so damn stubborn?

I clear my throat nervously. "A church, huh?"

"You don't have to come in, Eden. It means a lot to me that you came here at all. Even if you didn't know where you were going."

"It's fine," I reply shakily. I'm fine. This is fine. *Everything is fine.*

He opens his door, so I follow his lead, climbing out behind him. "So... why are we here?"

"When I was a kid, my father brought me to church here. Ma still lives just around the corner." He explains, turning around to point in the general direction as if I have any idea where we are.

"Okay," I reply as I stare up at the stone entrance that easily towers over everything within a hundred miles.

"When he kicked me out, this is where I came. There was a woman, Suzanne. She stayed up all night listening to me sob and explain what happened."

"She was nice?" I deduce.

"She took me home. I lived with her for two years until I could get on my own feet. She had my father banned from the church, which he was absolutely livid about, and she made this a safe place for me. Me and other kids like me."

"People like *us*? Gay?"

He looks over, giving me a weak smile as he reaches for my hand. "Yeah. People like us, Eden."

"Are we visiting her?"

"No, baby." He says as he shakes his head. "She died a few years ago. I come here on the anniversary of that first night. To pay my respect for her and as a middle finger to the man who left me for dead. I wouldn't be where I am without them. *Both of them.*"

I grip his hand tighter, trying to give him all of my strength. I don't need it today, anyway.

The closer we get to the entrance, the more I think that maybe I was wrong. Maybe I did need *some* of it. The stone overhang is probably as cold to the touch as it looks. The rocks and mortar are damp and dreary. A musty smell invades my lungs as Dixon drags open the solid wood door by the brass handle. We step directly into the main hall, the dim lights hardly illuminating the space. I imagine the hundreds, possibly thousands, of times a preacher has stood at the front of all these pews and spewed bullshit to anyone that would listen. My brain goes haywire, stuck on all the things I've been subjected to in my lifetime, and I scold myself for having such negative thoughts about a place that Dixon loves so dearly. I'm sure it wasn't like that here.

He heads straight for the front, but I take my time wandering down the center, my fingers trailing along the wooden pews with reverence. I take in the swirling pattern on the edges of the seats and immediately sense the familiarity.

"You made these," I announce as I look up at him. He gives me a weak smile over his shoulder before nodding. He turns back around, kneeling at the platform, so I quietly continue admiring his work while he pays his respects.

Today, his burdens are heavy, and when he stands to face me again, I feel like I should share some of myself with him. Maybe we can combine what we have weighing us down, and it'll be easier to carry together.

"I used to go to a church that looked a lot like this," I say as he walks toward me.

"Yeah?"

"Every Sunday," I agree as I walk over a few pews and sit down. "And quite a few Saturdays, actually. There were *a lot* of weddings."

"Really? That's kind of surprising."

"I remember the very first wedding I ever went to. I sat right here. Four pews from the front, right at the end." I admit as my cheeks heat.

Dixon walks over, taking my hand in his as he sits down next to me. I feel a lot stronger with him beside me, and I can't help but wonder... if we *were* created by God, did he make me that way on purpose? Did he create me for Dixon the way I believe he created him for me? Did God give him a big heart, a contagious smile, and soft touches while thinking 'Eden will need these'? I feel like he did.

"The groom was waiting at the front," I say as I point to the stage. "All of the pews were full, but everyone was so quiet. All I could hear was that awful music playing over the crackling speakers. There were ribbons, strings of pearls, and flower petals all down the aisle. I thought it was incredible. It felt so magical."

"I bet. How old were you?"

I shrug my shoulders noncommittally. "Seven. Eight, maybe." I admit as I look down at our fingers laced together. I can't help but smile despite the memory that I'm facing.

"When I looked at the groom, I imagined that I would be him someday. I'd be standing at the end of the aisle waiting for the person I loved more than anything in the world to meet me there."

I squeeze his hand a little tighter, grateful for the life we have together now. It still feels like a lot. At that time, I was so hopeful, and by the end of that night, I wasn't the same. Everything that felt magical, it had been stolen from me. That was the night they started carving me into the person they wanted me to be, not the person I was meant to be.

"I pictured a man," I admit with a sad chuckle. My eyes start to prickle, tears building around the edges of my vision.

"Eden," Dixon starts, but I hold up my hand to stop him.

"I... uh... My father wasn't there. Or he *was*, but he was off somewhere. With a girl, probably." I chuckle at the fact that it took me this long to realize where he was that day. "I tugged on my mother's sleeve and asked her if a man could walk down the aisle, because that's what I wanted. I knew that's how it was supposed to be for me. That was the only way it made sense." I say as I wipe at my eyes.

"She said no, of course. She said that only women were allowed to walk down the aisle and I was to never, *ever*, say something like that in front of my father. I didn't understand, because it didn't make sense. What was so bad about wanting a man to walk down the aisle?"

I pause for a second to gather myself before I continue, taking a deep breath and leaning back against the pew. "She dragged me out of the ceremony, all the way around the building until we were somewhere that no one could overhear us. She said," I pause to clear my throat. "She said that it didn't matter if I felt that way about boys or not, I was to never say anything about it. To anyone. That the way we lived, it wasn't allowed. I would be exiled, and I would never be able to see my family or friends again. I couldn't look at boys for too long, I couldn't talk about them to anyone, and most of all... if my father said I was to marry a woman, then that was what God had planned for me. I would do it. No questions asked, and I would never speak a word about that conversation either."

"No one should hear that, Eden. *Ever*."

"I know that," I agree. "Well, I know that *now*. It just felt really big back then, you know? I could feel every word from her mouth crumbling pieces of me. Like my soul shattering. It wasn't just that I couldn't talk about it... it was that she wasn't even admitting how wrong their opinions were. She just laid out the facts and left me to deal with all of those feelings on my own. I didn't know what I was doing. God," I sniffle. "I was just a child."

"I know, kid." He says as he pulls my head against his chest. "I know."

I find myself nodding, because if anyone could understand what I went through, it'd be him.

"You can have it now, though. If you want a guy to walk down the aisle, then you can have it. The preacher here would be happy to do it."

I smile before sitting up and looking backwards down the aisle. "You know how you come here in spite of your father?" I ask, turning back around.

"Yeah," he agrees as he pulls our linked hands into his lap.

"I think that's what I'm going to do," I admit. "I'm gonna be the one walking down the aisle. She said it couldn't be done. So, *I'm* gonna do it." I say with a weak smile.

He wraps his arm around my head, pulling me close enough to kiss the top of my head. We're both quietly soaking up the moment as he holds me against him. I can feel his lips curve into a smile before he kisses me again.

"I can't wait to see it, kid." He whispers.

Me either.

Chapter Twelve

Dixon

The roads are slick today, and I'm being a little extra cautious. Having someone waiting on you at home, it changes everything. You sleep a little easier with them by your side, but every move when you're apart, it's calculated. Careful. I need every minute I can get with him.

I round the bend and do a double take before pulling into the same parking lot I stop at on a regular basis. Sometimes with Eden, and sometimes alone. I'll sit here for hours and try to figure out what exactly he sees in *this* spot. There are better views higher on the mountain, there are quieter places a few roads over, there are even steeper peaks just a few miles away. What about this spot makes it *his* spot?

I slam the door closed, and he throws a hand out in my direction before I'm even close enough. I tug the pack of cigarettes from my pocket, sliding one between my lips before I offer one to him. Instead of grabbing it, he leans over and takes it between his lips. He doesn't move, waiting for me to light it. After a long inhale, he wraps his fingers around it and pulls it away from his lips.

"I was hoping you wouldn't find me today," he says as he looks down at the stupid fucking railing regretfully.

We're both quiet for a minute, letting the weight of his words sink in. "Why do you do it? Come here?"

There's a sad smile on his lips as he tilts his head toward the first rays of sunshine we've seen in days. "I can't stop it, Dixon. No matter how badly I want to. It's not just an itch I need to scratch. It's the universe pulling me to where it thinks I belong. The longer I fight it, the worse I feel. Just coming here, being in this spot, it settles something inside of me. It cleanses that tugging pressure just enough for me to get by."

"Do you think it'll ever go away? The desire?"

"I don't know, old man." He lets out a deep sigh as he shrugs. "*I don't know.*"

It's taken me far too long, months and months, to finally realize that I've gotten in way over my head. I have no idea what the fuck I'm doing with Eden. Not only is he just a kid, but it's not like we could ever be together. There's a lot of things that I'm willing to overlook, but trust isn't one of them. The sad part is that I could trust him to stay faithful. When it comes to other people, anyway. I have no doubt that his world would revolve around me, like I'm the goddamn sun. I just can't trust that he'd always choose me the way I would choose him. I can't trust that one day he wouldn't drive to this spot and choose it instead of me. I knew that this was a problem, but it hadn't really hit me *how much* of a problem it was until now.

To Eden, I'm not his ending. I'm not the person he's been searching his whole life for. I'm not even the person he wants to spend the *rest* of his life with. I'm just a fleeting moment of happiness before he gets to where he thinks he's meant to be, and something about that, it cuts deeper than anything I've ever felt before. I don't know how to explain what it feels like to love a person so wholly that you'd sacrifice anything for them and know that they wouldn't do the same for you.

I toss my cigarette butt to the ground and walk off. I can feel Eden's eyes on me as I slam the door closed and crank the truck.

I don't know what to say to him. I don't know what the fuck I've got myself into, and...

I sure as fuck don't know if I can keep doing this.

Chapter Thirteen

DIXON

I'm in the kitchen, starting breakfast when my phone rings. I'm so caught up in what I'm doing that I pick it up without even thinking, without even looking at it. I hear the sniffles on the other end of the line first, which is what gives away *who* called. The words out of her mouth, I expect them, but that doesn't make them land any softer.

"He's gone," she says with a quiet sob. "You need to come home, Dixon."

A silence settles between us as she awaits my reply, and I spend too long debating exactly what it's going to be. All my brain can focus on is the fact that I can hear Eden moving around upstairs, and it'll only be a few seconds before he's bouncing down the stairs to pester me while I finish cooking.

"I'll think about it," I reply before disconnecting the call and tossing my phone on the counter.

I didn't actually intend to think about it, but I do. All through breakfast and the entire time we drive over to the hardware store. I'm still thinking about it when the little bell over the door chimes and we step inside. I'm still thinking about it as Eden wanders off to look around at all the second-hand car parts while I head straight to the front desk. I assumed that I would still be thinking about it while the sweet little old man at the counter finished reading his article in the newspaper before acknowledging me... but I was wrong.

Right there on the front cover, there's an unassuming picture of the man I despise alongside a dainty little woman. It's him. I know it in the very marrow of my bones before I even read the headline. I glance over my shoulder, trying to discreetly locate Eden to make sure that he's not close enough to see it before turning back around to read the words boldly printed across the front.

Father Shane Arbor murdered in cold blood.

It's unmistakably him. He has the same eyes as Eden, they're just frigid and lifeless instead of full of wonder and joy. He has the same hair as Eden. Hair that I know is soft as silk because I've brushed my fingers through it hundreds of times. The freckles, the nose, all of it. They're almost twins except for their unmistakable age difference.

My first thought is of Eden, obviously. My second thought is good riddance. My third, well... it's that I highly doubt this was done in cold blood knowing the things I know. My thoughts don't stop there though, because of course not. *They can't.*

It's many seconds of silence later when I realize just how bad this is, *how scary it is*, because his parents... they're the only thing keeping him alive. I should be buckling up, readying myself to be a shoulder to lean on for someone that I care about in a moment of loss. That's what people do when they love someone, they're there for them. That's not what happens though. My eyes scan over the ridiculous article about this disgusting man, but my brain isn't processing any of the words. Instead of preparing myself to break the news of this loss to Eden, I panic. Full-blown, throw all my plans out the window, kind of panic.

I spin around on my heels, beelining for Eden. Forget the brackets for the cabinets. Forget the screws. Fuck it all. We have to get out of here. *Now.*

The television in the corner of the shop is blaring the news, and as soon as his picture is thrown up on the screen, I'm sure that Eden's going to hear them say his name. Nothing but pure panic and adrenaline are powering me as I manage to grab ahold of Eden and drag him back through the front door before we're both thrust into a situation that I am certain I could not survive.

"What the fuck?" He growls as he tries to jerk his arm away from me.

I ignore him as I head straight for the truck and open the door. I'm wasting no time. I have to get Eden out of this city before someone connects the dots and starts asking him questions, or before he sees it for himself.

"Let's go," I demand. He scowls at me as he stomps over to the truck and swings open the door.

"What is going on?" He asks as he slams the door closed behind him.

"They didn't have what we need. They're out of stock right now."

"They're out of screws?" He asks incredulously.

I crank the truck, sighing in frustration. I don't like lying to him. I don't like lying to anyone, but I don't know what else to do right now. "No, Eden. The screws don't help me if there aren't any brackets though, do they?"

He squints his eyes in suspicion, but he settles into his seat anyway.

"Can we go to the diner?" He asks as I turn out onto the main street that runs through the center of town.

"No," I reply sternly. "I'll make us something at home."

He eyes me again, this time it isn't with disbelief though, it's with disappointment. I can feel the chasm forming between us before he even speaks it into existence.

"Just take me home, Dixon." He says with a defeated sigh. "I don't feel good."

I pace around my kitchen and living room, but no matter how many steps I take, the *right* steps never come to me.

The fact that I love Eden does nothing but make this more complicated. When I found him on that cliffside, I never imagined that we'd end up where we are. I never thought that we would be inseparable. I never thought that a day would come where I'd have to make the choice on whether or not to give him a piece of information that could change his life, *our lives*, forever. I never thought that I would have to choose between doing the right thing or making a selfish choice to keep the person I love with me.

It shouldn't be a fucking choice.

I have all these options, all these paths, laid out in front of me, but they just look like some intricate puzzle. There's no yellow brick road to follow. No breadcrumb trails to lead the way. No matter which direction I go, this ends in a catastrophe.

Unfortunately for me, I'm a coward. I've *always* been a coward.

When there's a knock on the door, I don't expect it to be Eden. He never knocks. When I open the door and he's standing in front of me with tears in his eyes, I want to comfort him, but I don't. I already know that he's not mine to comfort anymore, if he *ever* was to begin with.

"We should talk," I say as if I was the one showing up on his front porch, stepping aside to let him in.

He quietly walks around me and takes his normal spot on my sofa. I don't sit.

"I'm sorry," he whispers. Which only makes me angry, because he hasn't done anything wrong. Not really.

"Sorry for what?" I ask as I pause my pacing to look over at him.

He shrugs noncommittally. "For making you angry this morning."

"You didn't make me angry, kid." I scoff. "The world made me angry."

He shifts on the sofa, keeping his eyes on anything other than me. I don't blame him. "I don't understand."

"Eden, I need you to tell me something, and I need you to be honest."

"Oh—Okay," he chokes out as his eyes cut to me. They aren't the same shade of happy that I love seeing on him. They're sad, *so sad*, and I know it's my fault. I thought that I helped Eden, but maybe I was wrong.

"What would happen if both of your parents died?"

His brows scrunch together in confusion, but he quickly rebounds, focusing on me instead. "I'd be happy, obviously."

"Yeah. And what about the cliff? Would you stop going there?"

He recoils, clearly disgusted by the idea. "We met there. Why would I—" He pauses, finally understanding where I'm going with this conversation. "I don't know, Dixon. I always thought that if they were gone then I would be free to— you know."

I'm not angry *at* him. I'm really not, but I *am* angry. I'm angry that God or the universe or whatever the fuck is out there is treating this like some fucking cosmic joke. It doesn't matter that Eden is the only person I care about, that he's the only person I've ever loved like this, the all-powerful is just as happy taking him away from me as it would be on any other Thursday afternoon. I don't know if this is his bad luck or mine, but it's somebodies.

"So what?" I growl. "Your hatred for them is the only thing you've ever lived for? Nothing else matters to you?"

He stares back at me, his lip quivering, and tears leaking down his cheeks. I want to be the one that takes this pain away from him, but I need to hear the truth. It's the only thing that can set us free, and as much as I hate the reality of this situation, I know that it can only end one way. The only hope I have of surviving this is being the person willing to walk away. Despite how small I feel in this moment, I *have* to be the bigger person. I have to make this decision for both of us.

"That was all I ever knew, Dixon." He whispers as he looks down at his hands, pulling them inside the sleeves of his hoodie.

"You keep saying *were* and *was*. What about now, Eden? I can't keep doing this! I live every fucking day for you. Hell, I would *die* for you, but it's not like that for you, is it?"

"Please don't do this," he begs as he looks up at me through his clumped lashes. "*Please, Dixon.*"

I run my hands through my hair, frustration pulsing through every vein. I didn't *want* to do this. I swear, I didn't.

I sit down on the loveseat across from him. "Eden... listen, kid."

"Stop. Calling. Me. That." He grits through his teeth.

I take a deep breath, sighing as I prop my elbows on my knees. "My father died, Eden." I say as I look up at him. "I'm taking a leave of absence from work to go help my mother. I'm gonna be gone for a little while."

"She likes me. I could come with you," he offers quietly, but there isn't any hope behind his words. He already knows what my answer is going to be. He already knows what's happening.

"I think we need to take a little time away from each other, Eden." I say as I hold my head between my palms. "This isn't healthy. For either of us."

He nods as he chews on his lip, letting himself digest everything I've said. He pauses, and then nods again, like everything makes sense, but it doesn't. None of it makes sense. How can you love a person this much, and still, both be sitting in a place that just doesn't work? How can you love a person *this fucking much*, and it not be enough?

He clears his throat. "Alright. Okay," he says as he gets to his feet. He wipes his eyes with the sleeves of his sweater and take a few steps toward the door. "Well... uh. I guess I'll see you when you get back. Give your mom my condolences."

"I will," I reply without looking up at him. I can't. I can't see his face. I can't see the pain I've caused him. *I can't stomach the mess I've made.*

He opens the door and closes it softly behind him. I wonder, not for the first time today, if this will be the last time I ever talk to Eden. Was this the last opportunity I ever had to see his face? Will I regret being a coward?

My heart isn't shattering into a million tiny pieces the way most people describe the pain of heartbreak. It isn't broken. It's just not. It still beats steadily in the chest of a boy I should've never loved. I can already feel him getting farther away, like without him nearby, I can't get enough oxygen in my blood. It's not painful in a normal sense. It's traumatizing. It's more like drowning, or self-induced poisoning. I know it's coming, I know what's happening, but I've done nothing to stop it.

I don't know how long I'm going to be gone. Days. Weeks. Months. No matter how long it is, I doubt he'll be here when I get back, but there's one question I can't stop asking myself. Where *will* he be? Will he have packed all his bags, sold a half-renovated house, and moved half-way across the country? Will he go a few towns over? A few states? Will he be close enough that I can still feel my heart beating in his chest when I lay in bed at night thinking about him? Or will my heart finally stop beating? Will he fill the inside of a silk lined coffin and end up just six feet away from me?

I consider never coming back, because I don't know if I can live with the answer.

Chapter Fourteen

EDEN

One Week Later

I pause, considering if I need another bottle or not. Ultimately, I don't think I could have too many, so I grab the bottle and put it in the buggy. The glass containers clank together loudly as I push the cart to the front of the shop. I swear to God, liquor companies need to reconsider their packaging. These bottles are too fucking noisy when you live in a constant state of hungover.

I stop at the counter, pulling each bottle from the shopping cart and sliding it onto the counter. I'm careful not to bang them against one another, but the cashier doesn't seem to have the same consideration. I pause, glaring over the counter at her until she gets the fucking idea. She starts moving slower, with a bit more caution, as she place the bottles in paper sacks, so I continue to unload my cart.

"A party?" She asks.

I eye her in annoyance. Do I actually look like I want to engage in small talk? It's probably my face. Forever this fucking baby face. I hate it. I've been here a couple times this week, and as much as I don't like this girl, she's the only person that never cards me, so I have to be grateful that she's here. I try to seem a bit more appreciative, just so that she doesn't quit or something ridiculous.

"Kind of," I say with a tired smile. *A pity party.*

Tomorrow is my twentieth birthday, and I expect to spend every second of it so drunk that I can't remember how fucking miserable I am. *Hooray.*

I get a carton of cigarettes along with what the cashier thinks is a party worth amount of liquor, and I go home.

It's quiet. *So quiet.* I think that's the worst part, honestly. I used to hear the sounds of the universe vibrating through me constantly. The birds, the frogs, the constant hum of the earth. It lived inside of my soul. For so long I believed that I was just this empty glass that sat around waiting to be filled, but as it turns out, I was wrong. I was wrong about a lot of things.

The truth was quite the opposite, it seems. I was so full of things that it was, at times, overwhelming, and I've only learned that because I actually know what it feels like to be empty now. It's worse, I think. I can't remember the last time I smiled, or laughed, or had a moment of true contentment. It feels like an eternity ago.

As I make trips back and forth from my kitchen to my jeep, I let the quiet wash over me. Maybe I can make friends with it, learn to hear the essence of it the way I used to with everything else, but all I hear is the stupid heart beating in my chest.

I turn on the stereo over my mantle so that I don't have to hear it anymore.

All day. I waited all day. I've texted him a dozen times this week, but I was sure that he would at least text me on my birthday.

I open the freezer and pull out the bottle to pour myself another glass. It's my fourth? Fifth? Who knows anymore. When the door of the freezer slams shut, it startles me, causing a bit of my drink to slosh over the edge of my cup.

"Well... that was a waste." I say as I glance down at the mess on the floor before glaring at the freezer like it's responsible for the disaster that is my life. Who knows? Maybe it is.

I step over the liquid on the floor, leaving it for another version of me to deal with, because this version of me? I don't give a fuck if the floor is sticky tomorrow. I walk over to the mantle, turning up the stereo, because if it's so quiet that the fridge scares me, then I obviously need more noise in here.

I go through another glass, and then another. Sometime around nine, maybe ten, my phone goes off. I expect it to be one of my five-thousand siblings that have been in contact with me regularly since my parents died, but when I pull out my phone. It's someone else. The words are blurry, both physically and in my brain.

Old Man:
> How are you, kid?

My first thought is pure anger. All the messages that I've sent him have gone ignored for a whole week. It's my fucking birthday. He called me that stupid name. He didn't fucking say anything important. *At all.* I want to reply with a lot of things. So many fucking things, but I'm sloshed, and the only thing that comes to mind is a smartass answer that I'm sure he'll get annoyed by. I know it's what he's really asking, the only thing he actually cares about, so I decide it's perfect.

Me:

I'm still alive.

Chapter Fifteen

Dixon

Two Weeks Later

"When do you plan on going home?" Ma asks as she clears off the stove. I take the dirty dishes to the sink, wondering if I can get away with ignoring her question altogether.

"Well?" She prods as she slings a rag over her shoulder.

"I don't know yet," I sigh. "I want to be here to help you for a little while. Make sure that you're doing alright. I don't like that you're going to be alone all the time."

"Your father was in an assisted living facility for years, son. I've been doing just fine on my own."

No matter how much she defends herself, she *hasn't* been doing good. I've heard that people can actually die of a broken heart, and I'm worried about her. Every day that passes she wakes up looking a little worse, a little less herself.

"You know what I mean, Ma." I argue as I grab the sponge and start washing the dishes.

"Have you talked to Eden?"

"Ma," I sigh as I plop my hands into the dishwater. We've already had this talk a dozen times, and I can assure you, talking about him *is not* helping me. At all.

"I'm not buying your bullshit, Dixon. You and that boy *are not* just friends, and I'm tired of hearing that same damn excuse every time I mention him."

"We *are* just friends, Ma." I demand as I spin around to stare at her. Well, we *were*.

"That boy looked at you the same way I looked at your father, Dixon. If you actually believe that the two of you were *just* friends, then you're dumber than a box of rocks." She says as she pulls the rag from her shoulder and starts wiping down the counter. I'm pretty sure that she already cleaned it. *Twice*. Did she forget?

"No, he didn't. We were only friends. Period. There's nothing else to the story, Ma."

"That boy loves you, Dixon."

"No, he doesn't, Ma! Please, drop it."

"Fine," she sighs. "Guess I'll be seeing you in Hell with the rest of us liars."

"See ya there," I retort. Hopeful that she's going to leave well enough alone, I turn back to the dishes.

When the lights are all off and I'm lying in bed, I toss and turn for hours the same way I've done every night for weeks. The bed is cold. The blankets are too thick. Too thin. It's too empty. There are too many pillows. It's too big. You name it, I've thought of it. I've used every excuse I can conjure up, but we all know the truth. It's just because he isn't in it.

I thought his ghost would only haunt my bed, my room, my house, but I couldn't have been more wrong. He's in everything I do, every move I make. I see him in everything and every place I go.

I do my best to fight the urge that's been itching at me. I deny myself every single day, except today.

Fridays are like the cheat days of a diet. I allow myself one message. Just one.

I pull out my phone, powering it on for the first time in a week. I ignore all the other messages from him, refusing to read any of them. I know I won't be able to stomach whatever he's had to say. I type out a message before back spacing and starting all over again. I want something that says I miss you and I can't stop thinking about you without saying any of that pathetic sounding shit.

Me:
> Ma wanted me to let you know that she's been thinking of you.

Eden:
> Oh yeah?

> Let her know that I've been thinking about her too.

> And that I'm still alive.

> It's a shame that she couldn't pick up the phone and tell me herself, you know?

I let out a sigh as I power the phone back off.
Coward.

Chapter Sixteen

EDEN

One Month Later

The ice cubes shift in the glass as I sit it on the counter. I refill it before going back to endless list of things I've made to keep myself busy. It's been almost two months. He can't stay gone forever, right?

I take a big swig before grabbing a cigarette and lighting it. Between the paint fumes and smoking, I decide to open the windows for a little while. The breeze feels pretty nice, too.

I pick up the roller and continue slathering on paint. Dark green looks nice with all the gold fixtures. Next on my list of things to do is learn how to make a bookshelf. Since Dixon isn't here, I doubt he'll give a fuck if I use his shop. I'm sure he has all the tools I need.

I scoff at the reminder of him, and the fact that it's already Friday. There's an itchiness inside of me when I think about him texting me later today. *Yet again.* Some days I look forward to it, it's *all* I can think about. Some days, like today, I almost resent the fact that he still does it. I constantly wonder what he could possibly get out of sending me one message a week, but I already know the answer to that, which is why I always give him the same reply.

Old Man:
How are you?

Me:
Still Alive.

I change his contact name in my phone to 'Asshole'. It makes me feel better for approximately five seconds before the novelty wears off. If the feeling I had in my chest before was love, I'm scared to know what the feeling in there now is.

Chapter Seventeen

DIXON

Three Months Later

"Where the hell have you been?" I demand as soon as Ma steps inside the front door. "I've been worried sick."

I rush over to help her inside. She's winded and definitely pushing herself too hard. She gives me an annoyed look as I grab her elbow and help her to the recliner in the living room. She swats at my hand just as we get close enough for her to sit down.

"You won't actually talk to the poor boy, so I went to see him myself."

I pause, completely confused... until I'm not. "Eden? You went to see Eden?"

"Who the hell else would I be talking about, son?" She rasps through labored breaths with a stern glare.

I recoil, stepping back from her. "*Ma.* Why would you do that? I told you to leave it alone."

She rolls her eyes as she scoots back in the chair and grabs the television remote. "It's no matter." She says with a flick of her wrist, waving the entire conversation away. "He wasn't there."

I eye her as she clicks through channels on the television. I already know that she's looking for the cooking channel, and normally I would help her get there, but my brain is too busy bouncing around in my skull.

"He wasn't home? Or he wasn't in Willows?"

"Neither I suppose. Least that's what the hairdresser said."

He left. He *actually* fucking left.

I take another step back from her, my stomach sinking. I don't know what I expected to happen.

That he'd stay there forever? That I'd always have the privilege of knowing where he was? I'd know what he was doing, that he was there missing me just as much as I was missing him? He's just a fucking kid. Did I really think he'd stick around pining over me for the rest of his life?

"I guess you were right. Maybe he didn't love you after all." She adds nonchalantly. Her eyes are locked on the television, so she's completely unaware of how I react physically to those words. How they cut so deep that all the blood is pouring out of my body, staining her Persian rug.

How did I not feel his absence? How did I not feel the way my heart wasn't close by anymore? It's so obvious now. The silence. The hole inside my chest that echoes my breaths. My entire existence, it means nothing without him.

How did I not know?

I stay up all night. Not that I would've been able to sleep, but as soon as the clock rolls over to midnight, I turn on my phone.

Me:

> **Are you okay?**

Eden:
> Fukkk Off
>
> I'm a teeny tinyyy bit drunk
>
> Or a bunch
>
> a bunch drunk

For the first time in almost five months, I debate sending a second message. I want to ask him where he went. I want to know if he's ever coming back. I want to know if he found out about his father dying. I want to know how he's been doing at his job. If he's still working at Buster's shop. I want to know how his day was. If he's been having trouble sleeping at night like I have. If he still thinks about me. *About us.*

Most of all, I want to know if he ever plans to return my heart.

I think I might already know the answer to that one though. So, I turn my phone off.

Chapter Eighteen

EDEN

Two Months Later

A hand slaps my shoulder, squeezing it a little tighter than it should. I spin around to find Evan looking over me as I work again. I was on a leave of absence for a few weeks so that I could attend the funerals and take care of some of the legal shit involving the investigation of my parent's murder. I missed coming to work. I was excited to get my hands dirty again, but I *did not* miss Evan.

Everything that Dixon said about him has been a lot more noticeable since he pointed it out. In fact, I've started to *not* like him because now that Dixon isn't around, he's been circling like a vulture. I find it irritating, honestly.

"I'm going out with the boys tonight. A gay bar a couple towns over. You interested?"

"No thanks," I grumble as I pull away from him. "I have shit to do before..." *he comes back.* I don't say the words, because I'm actually not sure if he's *ever* going to come back at this point. There are whispers around town, people are asking questions, making assumptions. It doesn't seem to matter if I said the words or not though, because Evan hears them.

"When *is* he coming back?" He asks with the same edge of disapproval that the rest of the town shares.

I spin around, glaring at him. "Why the fuck is it anyone's business? His father died, and his mother is on her own. He deserves time to handle the shit he needs to take care of. Why don't you all fuck off?"

"Hey," Evan says as he throws up his hands in innocence. "I didn't mean anything by it, Eden.

Maybe you could use a night to loosen up a little bit. Just have a couple drinks."

"I'm not changing my mind," I declare confidently as I squat back down and get back to work.

By eight o'clock, Dixon still hasn't texted me.

I go out with Evan and his friends.

The taxi drops us back off at my house after midnight. It's officially Saturday.

Dixon never texted me.

It feels wrong.

I'm starting to give up hope.

Chapter Nineteen

Dixon

One Week Later

August, an old friend of mine, steps up beside me. His face is solemn as he pats my shoulder sympathetically and takes the chair beside me. He doesn't offer empty words or comforts, and I appreciate that.

A week ago, I was having an argument with Ma in her kitchen. She had been demanding that I leave ever since she came back from her trip to Willows. According to her, I was just avoiding my problems. I argued with her until we were both blue in the face, but in hindsight, she was probably right.

The last thing she said to me that night was "I swear if you don't get out of my damn house and call that poor boy, I will find a way to make you leave, Dixon. So, help me, God."

It's kind of ironic, really, because I'm watching her casket be lowered into the ground today.

I guess she figured out how to get me to leave.

Chapter Twenty

Dixon

Two Months Later

I don't know what I expected, but when I noticed his jeep in the driveway, I had to knock. Suddenly, I had to *know*. No one answers the first time, so I knock again, but when the voice on the other side of the door isn't his, I debate turning around. I could run down the stairs and go back to my house, and I'd never know. I wouldn't have to see the proof of something I know I won't survive.

It's too late though. The door swings open, and of all people, Evan stares back at me. The stench of alcohol is overwhelming, and he's wearing nothing but underwear that are *very* unflattering.

"Evan?" I choke out bitterly.

I want to grab him by the throat and slam him against the wall. Not even a year has gone by, and he started clawing his way into Eden's life like some fucking stray cat, trying to replace me. I could literally strangle him, but as soon as that idea comes to mind, Eden stumbles out of his bedroom. His boxer's cling to his tiny body, and he looks just as perfect as I remember. A little smaller, a little skinnier, and I hope that's not my fault. It probably is. As much as I don't want to admit it, all of this is my fault.

The world changes like someone flipped on a switch in my brain. Colors seem brighter. Sounds that didn't register before, they're vibrating throughout my entire body. The closer he gets, the more I can feel my pulse coming back to life.

My heart is still in there. It's still beating.

"Look what the cat dragged in." Evan purrs as he steps back from the door, but I don't acknowledge him. I can't. My eyes are locked with Eden's, and that same tether that's always ran between us, it's just as strong as before. I can feel it pulling tighter with every step he takes. Without words, I try to tell him all the things I should've been saying over the last nine months. That I'm so fucking sorry. That I never meant to hurt him. That I miss what we had. I miss his laugh, his smile, his touch. *I miss him.*

I see a thousand things shining back at me in his eyes. For a moment, I'm hopeful that he feels the same way, that he's spent every minute thinking of me too. I can feel pain and remorse pouring off of him in waves, and I can't wait to tell him that everything is okay. That all of this is my fault. That I still love him. That I'll *always* love him.

I'd been carrying around that stupid fucking hope my entire life like it was running through my veins, but somehow, I'd let doubt creep in and run rampant. I care about Eden so much that the helplessness I felt sometimes, it chewed through my resolve. It created this imaginary barrier that never should've been there, because I've learned that no amount of distance or time will stop me from thinking of him. In my universe, it will always be Eden. *Always.*

He's my religion. My *only* salvation.

I'm pretty sure he wasn't thinking any of the things I was, though, because he grabs the solid wood door and slams it in my face.

Two days later, I'm still mulling over the disaster that is my life and how I intend to fix it, when I decide to go to the coffee shop. It's not like I've really slept in months, and all the food in my house is either gone or expired. Caffeine and a pastry seem like a lifeline that I probably don't deserve.

It's clear that the universe feels the same way, because as soon as I round the corner, the herringbone bricks beneath my feet nearly collapse in on themselves, dragging me straight to hell with them.

Right in front of me, in the coffee shop, stands Eden. A pretty little boy, probably a couple years younger than him, clings to his arm. Somehow, he's even smaller than Eden, and he fits perfectly against his side. There's a longing, and ache so deep in my bones, that I don't know how I'll ever move past this. *Past him.* It's not Evan, so that's a slight improvement, but when the boy smiles up at Eden with nothing but adoration on his face, it's not just the bricks that start caving in. It's my entire world.

I did this to myself, I think.

Me:
We should talk.

No reply.

> **Me:**
> It's been a week, Eden.
> We really need to talk.

Still... no answer.

> **Me:**
> Eden...
> Please?

Chapter Twenty-One

EDEN

There's only one logical place to go when I can't stop thinking about him. So, just before sunset, I start up the mountain. I have the doors off the jeep for the first time in almost a year. The wind whips around, my hair flying in all directions. The smell of pine trees and crisp mountain streams flood my lungs, and it feels so nostalgic that my insides ache. I've been here so many times over the last nine months, but it hasn't felt like this in such a long time. It's like coming home after almost a year of being lost at sea.

The gravel crunches beneath my tires as I turn into the parking lot that's always empty, except it *isn't* empty today. For a second, I debate leaving. Just turning around the vehicle and riding back down the mountain, but I know the truth of this situation. No matter how much I try to avoid him, Willows is a small town, and eventually I'll have to face this.

I park my jeep beside his truck and take a deep breath before I force myself to climb out. I pause before fully rounding the front of the vehicle and just take him in. He doesn't tear his eyes away from the horizon, and I can feel all the longing and pain radiating off of him.

He looks older. In just nine months, I can see the toll the world has taken on him. The silver at his temples has spread farther, and he wears his exhaustion like battle wounds. He's still handsome, in a worn rugged way, but he isn't the Dixon I used to know. I wonder, for the first time, if this feeling inside of me is what he always felt when he'd find me here. If he knew that there was nothing he could really do or say to change the outcome of things, but that he wished things were different. *I wish things were different.*

"You're in my spot, old man."

He finally turns to look at me, a flicker of a sad smile rising on his lips before it disappears completely.

"I'll go—" He starts, but I step toward him, holding out a cigarette from my shirt pocket.

"Stay," I offer. *I practically beg*.

As much as I've avoided him, I miss this. Us being here together. It got harder and harder to come here without him. This is the place that feels like… us. His smiles, his laughs, *his love*, this is the place where I felt them all first.

He takes the cancer stick from me and slides over, giving me room to hop up beside him on the hood of his truck. I climb up beside him, lighting my cigarette before offering the lighter to him.

"I hated this place," he starts before blowing out a trail of smoke. "For so long."

"I could never hate this place," I whisper.

He looks over at me, just for a second, but now that I'm closer to him it's easy to see the trail down his face where the salt from tears have dried to his skin. I glance down at my hands, knowing that I'm the reason those tears were there, and hating myself for it. I could've been braver, *should've been*, and it probably would've saved *both* of us a lot of pain.

He flicks the ashes from his cigarette before looking back up at the sinking sun. "I knew it'd take you away from me someday. I just didn't know that I'd play a part in it, you know? I didn't know it'd be like *this*."

I want to tell him everything. That I haven't thought about that in a long time. That it doesn't have to be like this anymore. That I don't *want* it to be.

When he left, I spent a lot of time trying to figure out why. I didn't understand how he could feel the way I felt and imagine that living without what we had would be easier than living with it. It took a lot of drinking and a lot of thinking to see the truth. It took me even longer to see that the elephant in the room was always me. He gave me everything, and I only gave him part of myself. It was never fair, and I know that now.

Am I mad that he avoided me and disappeared for so long? Absolutely. That hurt just as bad, if not worse, than him leaving in the first place, but in a way, I'm grateful for the time we've had apart. In just nine months, I feel like a completely different person. I'm not the boy I was when Dixon and I met, but I think I'm okay with that. Maybe even proud of it.

"They're both dead now," I admit as I toss the filter to the ground. "Since the week you left. I only come up here now when I'm thinking about us."

"Yeah?" He asks with a sad chuckle as he looks down at his cigarette before tossing it beside mine.

I scoot closer, leaning my head against his shoulder. "Yeah," I reply on an exhale. "Days like today."

He wraps his arm around me, pulling me as close as he can before softly kissing the top of my head. "I missed you, kid." He whispers.

I smile softly. "I missed you too, old man."

THE END

Attention!

The first thing I want to make very clear is that Eden's dependency on someone else to make him feel like he needed to stay alive did not just disappear. In a perfect world, dealing with mental illnesses would be that simple, but that's not how reality works. All Eden did was transfer that responsibility to Dixon. As I mentioned before, these are not healthy ways to deal with his mental illnesses or trauma, but they are *realistic* ways that people deal with them. It's not something to strive for, it's not poetic, and it's not romantic. The parts of their relationship that were healthy, where they opened up to one another and adored the presence of the other no matter their broken pieces, that's romance. The trauma, the struggling, the suffering, those are far too common, and far too overlooked. Reach out to your family, your friends, even your acquaintances. Be the person that helps them find the resources they need to overcome their struggles. Be the difference.

If you want to catch some glimpses of where Eden and Dixon end up in the future, and what they've been getting up after their reunion, don't forget to join me for the next book in The Namesake Series.

TAKE A SNEAK PEEK AT:

August

Will

Present Day

I tug at the tie around my neck, certain it's tied to tight. Everyone has already taken their seats, and the god-awful music is blaring overhead. As if being around this many people isn't enough to induce a panic attack, I'm in a room full of people I *know*. Siblings, friends, acquaintances. People that will likely want to talk as soon as the ceremony is over. Just thinking about it has me breaking out in a sweat.

Eden said that he'd understand if I wanted to leave before the reception, but I owe him and Dixon for all the help they given me. I really don't want to disappoint them.

I shift nervously as I glance across the stage in search of the only person aside from the men of the hour that has the ability to ground me.

August.

His honey brown eyes are already on me, most likely assessing the level of distress I'm in. It's like he has a radar for the shit. He can sniff out my discomfort the way a hound can trail a coon. His hands are clasped in front of him and he gestures with them, reminding me of what I should be focused on.

The wedding.

It's hard though. *Really fucking hard.* Especially when the church we're standing in is remarkably similar to the one back… there. The place I've been trying, *and failing*, to forget about.

August was a frequent customer at Buster's. His regular trips to the shop had him and Eden becoming quick friends. Even if that weren't the case, he was already good friends with Dixon. Which is why he's standing across the stage from me right now instead of beside me.

They were supposedly really close in high school, but lost touch when Dixon moved out of town. As the story goes, they reconnected at Betty's funeral and Dixon told him about Willows. A couple weeks later, he had rented a place there, and it's now his permanent home. One where I can never seem to avoid running into him. Not that I try.

This place has really grown over the last year or two. For some reason, a lot of our siblings have seemed to flock to Eden. I don't know if it's because he's actually got his shit together or if it's because he was the only one that was ever brave enough to leave that shithole *before* our parents died. To be honest, it's probably because the government seized all our family's assets and we were left with nothing. Once my siblings found out that Eden had inherited a fuck ton of money from our grandparents after he left... Well, most of them have made their way to *or* near Willows. I don't even like thinking that though, because Eden is such a good fucking person and he genuinely cares about all of us.

Dixon comes down the aisle, taking his place between August and me, as he waits on Buster to walk Eden down the aisle. As soon as Eden is in view, Dixon's eyes start to grow misty.

I've been attached to Eden's hip since the day our parents died. He'd been pretty torn up about Dixon being gone at the time, and I never really understood. Love wasn't really a thing where we came from, but it's something I've definitely witnessed now. The relationship I've watched blossom between them is practically addictive. There's so much adoration pouring off of them that it's almost like you soak some of it up for yourself just by being around them.

When I glance over at August again, he scowls at me with the same disapproval he always seems to have for me these days. I hate that his presence comforts me almost as much as I appreciate it. He just doesn't seem to like me, but that wasn't always the case. I clear my throat, trying to choke back the memories, because they don't matter anymore. What matters is *right now,* and now, August avoids me as much as possible. Unfortunately, I appear to be the *only* person he loathes with a fiery passion.

Which is even more obvious after the grooms kiss and the reception kicks off. August wanders around the room, happy to entertain a seemingly endless number of guests. My eyes constantly seek him out, longing for the comfort he offers, as I nurse a lone glass of champagne from my seat in the back corner of the room. His name card is right next to mine at the table, but he hasn't come over here a single time.

I don't even have to look to know where he's at in the mass of people. I can pinpoint his laughter even through the symphony of other chatter in the room. It's husky and deep... and completely elusive. For me anyway. He never laughs when I'm around anymore, and I wish I could figure out why.

I startle, ripping my eyes away from him, when Eden plops down in his seat beside me. His hair is sweaty, and his breaths come out fast and heavy from all the dancing he's been doing. I wish I had his endless energy.

"Thanks for sticking around," he says as he ruffles my hair lovingly. "Having you here means a lot, Will."

Eden and I weren't nearly as close when we were younger, because we didn't really have the time to be, but I was closest to him out of all our siblings. Which is why I clung to him when our parents died, but now, the bond between us is indescribable.

"Of course. I wouldn't miss it," I reply honestly.

"So," he starts as he leans forward to steal my glass of champagne. "Any ideas for what you wanna do yet?"

I look away, mainly to avoid any hint of disappointment on his face when I answer, but my eyes wander around the room. The dozens of people milling about, enjoying the festivities. They flourish in the presence of other people. The fairy lights strung around the room flicker in their eyes as they excitedly chat with everyone else. There are at least a dozen people out on the makeshift dance floor with Dixon. More of them congregate at the open bar. There are a few tables of people that are content conversing among one another, but I'm the only person that's alone. Certainly, the only person that *prefers* to be alone.

My eyes find August again, drinking in his magnetic charm as he animatedly tells a story to Cameron and Callie in a way that even seems to be entertaining the toddler clinging to Cam's leg.

On a night that's magical to everyone else in attendance, one thing becomes blatantly clear.

"I don't belong here, Eden." I sigh, almost in relief, as I take my glass back from him.

"Will." He starts, but I cut him off.

"I'm gonna leave Willows," I decide. "Maybe find a cabin or something close by."

He looks pained by my admission, but he nods anyway. Over the last few months he's had a front row seat to my social anxiety. It's not circumstantial, and it's not improving. Even with therapy. Some things just can't be fixed. Some *people* just can't be fixed.

"I might have the perfect idea. We'll get together after the honeymoon, okay?" He urges anxiously, as if I'm going to run off in the next nine days.

Despite my apprehension, I give him an appreciative smile, nodding in agreement.

"Perfect," he says as he hops from his seat, his eyes immediately finding his husband. The love and happiness that pours off of him leaves a flicker of yearning in my gut.

He turns back to me. "August said he'd take you home. I'll let him know you're ready, Okay?"

"Nah, he's having a good time." I insist as I glance over at him again. His eyes lock with mine across the room, but I turn away almost immediately, facing Eden instead.

"I've already got a taxi on the way," I lie.

Acknowledgements

There are a lot of things I could say about Eden, Dixon, and their relationship, but I don't think I will. From the moment they popped in my head, their story was never meant to be easy. I knew they would hurt, and I knew they would struggle to find who they were. Both on their own, and together. I knew there would be unanswered questions, but I like that about them. From the way Eden's world was in HD when he was with Dixon, to the way it became greyscale while they were apart. The very real, and very painful fears that Dixon had, to learning how to cope with them when faced with the alternative. There is so much depth to these characters that I'll never be able to voice. Even if I had the words, I don't think I would. I like that their ending is... *theirs*. You'll still get to see little glimpses of them and how their life develops in the future. If you're looking forward to seeing more of them, be sure to follow me on socials to get all the teasers for the upcoming books in The Namesake Series!

To my husband: Any form of genuine love reminds me of you. The good, the bad, the pretty, the ugly, the easy, the hard, all of it, because to be honest, love comes in every form. After all these years together, I've learned that sometimes we see sides of the people we love that aren't very pretty. Sometimes we *give* sides of ourselves that aren't pretty either but finding someone that accepts us anyway... that's the true beauty of love. That's what I've found with you. If there is a God out there, you're what I'd thank him for.

Lydia, you know these boys were for you. I sent you the very first ideas I had for these two, and you immediately claimed them. You wanted to see them brought to life, so I let them lead the way. They gave us a story that I will never forget, and in a way, I have you to thank for that. I hope they held your heart exactly the way you wanted. And I love you.

To anyone that reads this: I hold this story extremely close to my chest. It's my favorite thing I've written so far, and at the point in time that I'm writing this, I don't know if I'll even share this story with the world. It's short and it's a little painful. It's *a lot* in a short amount of time. If you see this, then I decided it was worth it. I sincerely hope you thought so, too.

To the other people I love. Especially Eddie. Thank you for taking the time to read over this when your life was chaos. I hope you and Cody know that no number of miles between us could change how much I love you both. You're the best.

Mom, for never crying when I ask you to print a million things for me. Your support may be silent, but it's not unheard.

And because I know everyone is thinking the exact same thing... The boy that Dixon saw Eden with in the coffee shop, that was Will. He's one of Eden's (many) younger brothers. His book is *August*, and it's in the works! ;)

J. Wilhelm is from the deep, *deep*, south. She's a parent to a sweet little girl, a greyhound, and a husband. She tends not to take life too seriously and spends most of her free time in imaginary worlds. (Whether that be writing, reading, or video games.) She takes pride in being a treasure trove of completely useless knowledge, especially regarding science topics. She really enjoys romance novels and may or may not have an *extremely* large collection of books that borders on insane. If you need more information or want to chat, reach out to jpwilhelmwriting@gmail.com.